# ACROSS THE BRIDGE

*Stories*

*by*

*Mavis Gallant*

Random House   New York

Library of Congress Cataloging-in-Publication Data
Gallant, Mavis.
Across the bridge : short stories / by Mavis Gallant. — 1st
ed.
p.   cm.
Contents: Déclassé — The chosen husband — From cloud to cloud —
Florida — Dédé — Kingdom come — Across the bridge — Forain —
A state of affairs — Mlle. de Corta — The Fenton Child.
ISBN 0-679-42213-7 :
I. Title
PR9199.3.G26A64 1993
813'.54—dc20          92-27270

*Book design by Tanya M. Pérez*

Manufactured in the United States of America
24689753
First Edition

To
Kitty Crowe

# Contents

# ACROSS THE BRIDGE

# 1933

About a year after the death of M. Carette, his three survivors—Berthe and her little sister, Marie, and their mother—had to leave the comfortable flat over the furniture store in Rue Saint-Dennis and move to a smaller place. They were not destitute: there was the insurance and the money from the sale of the store, but the man who had bought the store from the estate had not yet paid and they had to be careful.

Some of the lamps and end tables and upholstered chairs were sent to relatives, to be returned when the little girls grew up and got married. The rest of their things were carried by two small, bent men to the second floor of a stone house in Rue Cherrier near the Institute for the Deaf and Dumb. The men used an old horse and an open cart for the removal. They told Mme. Carette that they had never worked outside that quarter; they knew only some forty streets of Montreal but knew them thoroughly. On moving day, soft snow, like graying lace, fell. A patched tarpaulin protected the Carettes' wine-red sofa with its border of silk fringe, the children's brass bedstead, their mother's walnut bed with the carved scallop shells, and the round oak table, smaller than the old one, at which they would now eat their meals. Mme. Carette told Berthe that her days of entertaining and cooking for guests were over. She was just twenty-seven.

They waited for the moving men in their new home, in scrubbed, empty rooms. They had already spread sheets of *La Presse* over the floors, in case the men tracked in snow. The curtains were hung, the cream-colored blinds pulled halfway down the sash windows. Coal had been delivered and was piled in the lean-to shed behind the kitchen. The range and the squat, round heater in the dining room issued tidal waves of dense metallic warmth.

The old place was at no distance. Parc Lafontaine, where the children had often been taken to play, was just along the street. By walking an extra few minutes, Mme. Carette could patronize the same butcher and grocer as before. The same horse-drawn sleighs would bring bread, milk, and coal to the door. Still, the quiet stone houses, the absence of heavy traffic and shops made Rue Cherrier seem like a foreign country.

Change, death, absence—the adult mysteries—kept the children awake. From their new bedroom they heard the clang of the first streetcar at dawn—a thrilling chord, metal on metal, that faded slowly. They would have jumped up and dressed at once, but to their mother this was still the middle of the night. Presently, a new, continuous sound moved in the waking streets, like a murmur of leaves. From the confused rustle broke distinct impressions: an alarm clock, a man speaking, someone's radio. Marie wanted to talk and sing. Berthe had to invent stories to keep her quiet. Once she had placed her hand over Marie's mouth and been cruelly bitten.

They slept on a horsehair mattress, which had a summer and a winter side, and was turned twice a year. The beautiful stitching at the edge of the sheets and pillows was their mother's work. She had begun to sew her trousseau at the age of eleven; her early life was spent in preparation for a wedding. Above the girls' bed

4

hung a gilt crucifix with a withered spray of box hedge that passed for the Easter palms of Jerusalem.

Marie was afraid to go to the bathroom alone after dark. Berthe asked if she expected to see their father's ghost, but Marie could not say: she did not yet know whether a ghost and the dark meant the same thing. Berthe was obliged to get up at night and accompany her along the passage. The hall light shone out of a blue glass tulip set upon a column painted to look like marble. Berthe could just reach it on tiptoe; Marie not at all.

Marie would have left the bathroom door open for company, but Berthe knew that such intimacy was improper. Although her First Communion was being delayed because Mme. Carette wanted the two sisters to come to the altar together, she had been to practice confession. Unfortunately, she had soon run out of invented sins. Her confessor seemed to think there should be more: he asked if she and her little sister had ever been in a bathroom with the door shut, and warned her of grievous fault.

On their way back to bed, Berthe unhooked a calendar on which was a picture of a family of rabbits riding a toboggan. She pretended to read stories about the rabbits and presently both she and Marie fell asleep.

They never saw their mother wearing a bathrobe. As soon as Mme. Carette got up she dressed herself in clothes that were in the colors of half-mourning—mauve, dove-gray. Her fair hair was brushed straight and subdued under a net. She took a brush to everything—hair, floors, the children's elbows, the kitchen chairs. Her scent was of Baby's Own soap and Florida Water. When she bent to kiss the children, a cameo dangled from a chain. She trained the girls not to lie, or point, or gobble their food, or show their legs above the knee, or leave fingerprints on windowpanes, or handle the parlor curtains—the slightest touch could crease the lace, she said. They learned to say in English, "I don't understand" and "I don't know" and "No, thank you." That was all the English anyone needed between Rue Saint-Denis and Parc Lafontaine.

In the dining room, where she kept her sewing machine, Mme.

Carette held the treadle still, rested a hand on the stopped wheel. "What are you doing in the parlor?" she called. "Are you touching the curtains?" Marie had been spitting on the window and drawing her finger through the spit. Berthe, trying to clean the mess with her flannelette petticoat, said, "Marie's just been standing here saying 'Saint Marguerite, pray for us.'"

Downstairs lived M. Grosjean, the landlord, with his Irish wife and an Airedale named Arno. Arno understood English and French; Mme. Grosjean could only speak English. She loved Arno and was afraid he would run away: he was a restless dog who liked to be doing something all the time. Sometimes M. Grosjean took him to Parc Lafontaine and they played at retrieving a collapsed and bitten tennis ball. Arno was trained to obey both "Cherchez!" and "Go fetch it!" but he paid attention to neither. He ran with the ball and Mme. Grosjean had to chase him.

Mme. Grosjean stood outside the house on the back step, just under the Carettes' kitchen window, holding Arno's supper. She wailed, "Arno, where have you got to?" M. Grosjean had probably taken Arno for a walk. He made it a point never to say where he was going: he did not think it a good thing to let women know much.

Mme. Grosjean and Mme. Carette were the same age, but they never became friends. Mme. Carette would say no more than a few negative things in English ("No, thank you" and "I don't know" and "I don't understand") and Mme. Grosjean could not work up the conversation. Mme. Carette had a word with Berthe about Irish marriages: An Irish marriage, while not to be sought, need not be scorned. The Irish were not English. God had sent them to Canada to keep people from marrying Protestants.

That winter the girls wore white leggings and mittens, knitted by their mother, and coats and hats of white rabbit fur. Each of them carried a rabbit muff. Marie cried when Berthe had to go to school. On Sunday afternoons they played with Arno and M. Grosjean. He tried to take their picture but it wasn't easy. The girls stood on the front steps, hand-in-hand, mitten-to-mitten, while Arno was harnessed to a sled with curved runners. The red harness had once been worn by another Airedale, Ruby, who was smarter even than Arno.

M. Grosjean wanted Marie to sit down on the sled, hold the reins and look sideways at the camera. Marie clung to Berthe's coat. She was afraid that Arno would bolt into the Rue Saint-Denis, where there were streetcars. M. Grosjean lifted her off the sled and tried the picture a different way, with Berthe pretending to drive and Marie standing face-to-face with Arno. As soon as he set Marie on her feet, she began to scream. Her feet were cold. She wanted to be carried. Her nose ran; she felt humiliated. He got out his handkerchief, checked green and white, and wiped her whole face rather hard.

Just then his wife came to the front door with a dish of macaroni and cut-up sausages for Arno. She had thrown a sweater over her cotton housecoat; she was someone who never felt the cold. A gust of wind lifted her loose hair. M. Grosjean told her that the kid was no picnic. Berthe, picking up English fast, could not have repeated his exact words, but she knew what they meant.

Mme. Carette was still waiting for the money from the sale of the store. A brother-in-law helped with the rent, sending every month a generous postal order from Fall River. It was Mme. Carette's belief that God would work a miracle, allowing her to pay it all back. In the meantime, she did fine sewing. Once she was hired to sew a trousseau, working all day in the home of the bride-to-be. As the date of the wedding drew near she had to stay overnight.

Mme. Grosjean looked after the children. They sat in her front parlor, eating fried-egg sandwiches and drinking cream soda (it did not matter if they dropped crumbs) while she played a record of a man singing, "Dear one, the world is waiting for the sunrise."

Berthe asked, in French, "What is he saying?" Mme. Grosjean answered in English, "A well-known Irish tenor."

When Mme. Carette came home the next day, she gave the girls a hot bath, in case Mme. Grosjean had neglected their elbows and heels. She took Berthe in her arms and said she must never tell anyone their mother had left the house to sew for strangers. When she grew up, she must not refer to her mother as a seamstress, but say instead, "My mother was clever with her hands."

That night, when they were all three having supper in the kitchen, she looked at Berthe and said, "You have beautiful hair." She sounded so tired and stern that Marie, eating mashed potatoes and gravy, with a napkin under her chin, thought Berthe must be getting a scolding. She opened her mouth wide and started to howl. Mme. Carette just said, "Marie, don't cry with your mouth full."

Downstairs, Mme. Grosjean set up her evening chant, calling for Arno. "Oh, where have you got to?" she wailed to the empty backyard.

"The dog is the only thing keeping those two together," said Mme. Carette. "But a dog isn't the same as a child. A dog doesn't look after its masters in their old age. We shall see what happens to the marriage after Arno dies." No sooner had she said this than she covered her mouth and spoke through her fingers: "God forgive my unkind thoughts." She propped her arms on each side of her plate, as the girls were forbidden to do, and let her face slide into her hands.

Berthe took this to mean that Arno was doomed. Only a calamity about to engulf them all could explain her mother's elbows on the table. She got down from her chair and tried to pull her mother's hands apart, and kiss her face. Her own tears ran into her long hair, down onto her starched piqué collar. She felt tears along her nose and inside her ears. Even while she

8

sobbed out words of hope and comfort (Arno would never die) and promises of reassuring behavior (she and Marie would always be good) she wondered how tears could flow in so many directions at once.

Of course, M. Grosjean did not know that all the female creatures in his house were frightened and lonely, calling and weeping. He was in Parc Lafontaine with Arno, trying to play go-fetch-it in the dark.

# THE CHOSEN HUSBAND

In 1949, a year that contained no other news of value, Mme. Carette came into a legacy of eighteen thousand dollars from a brother-in-law who had done well in Fall River. She had suspected him of being a Freemason, as well as of other offenses, none of them trifling, and so she did not make a show of bringing out his photograph; instead, she asked her daughters, Berthe and Marie, to mention him in their prayers. They may have, for a while. The girls were twenty-two and twenty, and Berthe, the elder, hardly prayed at all.

The first thing that Mme. Carette did was to acquire a better address. Until now she had kept the Montreal habit of changing her rented quarters every few seasons, a conversation with a landlord serving as warranty, rent paid in cash. This time she was summoned by appointment to a rental agency to sign a two-year lease. She had taken the first floor of a stone house around the corner from the church of Saint Louis de France. This was her old parish (she held to the network of streets near Parc Lafontaine) but a glorious strand of it, Rue Saint-Hubert.

Before her inheritance Mme. Carette had crept to church, eyes lowered; had sat where she was unlikely to disturb anyone whose life seemed more fortunate, therefore more deserving, than her own. She had not so much prayed as petitioned. Now she ran a glove along the pew to see if it was dusted, straightened the unread pamphlets that called for more vocations for missionary service in Africa, told a confessor that, like all the prosperous, she was probably without fault. When the holy-water font looked mossy, she called the parish priest and had words with his housekeeper, even though scrubbing the church was not her job. She still prayed every day for the repose of her late husband, and the unlikelier rest of his Freemason brother, but a tone of briskness caused her own words to rattle in her head. Church was a hushed annex to home. She prayed to insist upon the refinement of some request, and instead of giving thanks simply acknowledged that matters used to be worse.

Her daughter Berthe had been quick to point out that Rue Saint-Hubert was in decline. Otherwise, how could the Carettes afford to live here? (Berthe worked in an office and was able to pay half the rent.) A family of foreigners were installed across the road. A seamstress had placed a sign in a ground-floor window—a sure symptom of decay. True, but Mme. Carette had as near neighbors a retired opera singer and the first cousins of a city councillor—calm, courteous people who had never been on relief. A few blocks north stood the mayor's private dwelling, with a lamppost on each side of his front door. (During the recent war the mayor had been interned, like an enemy alien. No one quite remembered why. Mme. Carette believed that he had refused an invitation to Buckingham Palace, and that the English had it in for him. Berthe had been told that he had tried to annex Montreal to the State of New York and that someone had minded. Marie, who spoke to strangers on the bus, once came home with a story about Fascist views; but as she could not spell "Fascist," and did not know if it was a kind of landscape or something to eat, no one took her seriously. The mayor had eventually been released, was promptly reelected, and continued to add lustre to Rue Saint-Hubert.)

Mme. Carette looked out upon long façades of whitish stone, windowpanes with bevelled edges that threw rainbows. In her childhood this was how notaries and pharmacists had lived, before they began to copy the English taste for freestanding houses, blank lawns, ornamental willows, leashed dogs. She re-called a moneyed aunt and uncle, a family of well-dressed, soft-spoken children, heard the echo of a French more accurately expressed than her own. She had tried to imitate the peculiarity of every syllable, sounded like a plucked string, had tried to make her little girls speak that way. But they had rebelled, re-fused, said it made them laughed at.

When she had nothing to request, or was tired of repeating the same reminders, she shut her eyes and imagined her funeral. She was barely forty-five, but a long widowhood strictly observed had kept her childish, not youthful. She saw the rosary twined round her hands, the vigil, the candles perfectly still, the hillock of wreaths. Until the stunning message from Fall River, death had been her small talk. She had never left the subject, once entered, without asking, "And what will happen then to my poor little Marie?" Nobody had ever taken the question seri-ously except her Uncle Gildas. This was during their first Christ-mas dinner on Rue Saint-Hubert. He said that Marie should pray for guidance, the sooner the better. God had no patience with last-minute appeals. (Uncle Gildas was an elderly priest with limited social opportunities, though his niece believed him to have wide and worldly connections.)

"Prayer can fail," said Berthe, testing him.

Instead of berating her he said calmly, "In that case, Berthe can look after her little sister."

She considered him, old and eating slowly. His cassock ex-haled some strong cleaning fluid—tetrachloride; he lived in a rest home, and nuns took care of him.

Marie was dressed in one of Berthe's castoffs—marine-blue

velvet with a lace collar. Mme. Carette wore a gray-white dress Berthe thought she had seen all her life. In her first year of employment Berthe had saved enough for a dyed rabbit coat. She also had an electric seal, and was on her way to sheared raccoon. "Marie had better get married," she said.

Mme. Carette still felt cruelly the want of a husband, someone—not a daughter—to help her up the step of a streetcar, read *La Presse* and tell her what was in it, lay down the law to Berthe. When Berthe was in adolescence, laughing and whispering and not telling her mother the joke, Mme. Carette had asked Uncle Gildas to speak as a father. He sat in the parlor, in a plush chair, all boots and cassock, knees apart and a hand on each knee, and questioned Berthe about her dreams. She said she had never in her life dreamed anything. Uncle Gildas replied that anyone with a good conscience could dream events pleasing to God; he himself had been doing it for years. God kept the dreams of every living person on record, like great rolls of film. He could have them projected whenever he wanted. Montreal girls, notoriously virtuous, had his favor, but only up to a point. He forgave, but never forgot. He was the embodiment of endless time—though one should not take "embodiment" literally. Eternal remorse in a pit of flames was the same to him as a rap on the fingers with the sharp edge of a ruler. Marie, hearing this, had fainted dead away. That was the power of Uncle Gildas.

Nowadays, shrunken and always hungry, he lived in retirement, had waxed linoleum on his floor, no carpet, ate tapioca soup two or three times a week. He would have stayed in bed all day, but the nuns who ran the place looked upon illness as fatigue, fatigue as shirking. He was not tired or lazy; he had nothing to get up for. The view from his window was a screen of trees. When Mme. Carette came to visit—a long streetcar ride, then a bus—she had just the trees to look at: she could not stare at her uncle the whole time. The trees put out of sight a busy commercial garage. It might have distracted him to watch trucks backing out, perhaps to witness a bloodless accident. In the morning he went downstairs to the chapel, ate breakfast, sat on his bed after it was made. Or crossed the gleaming floor to a small table, folded back the oilcloth cover, read the first sentence of a memoir he was writing for his great-nieces: "I was born in Montreal, on the 22nd of May, 1869, of pious Christian parents, connected to Montreal families for whom streets and bridges have been named." Or shuffled out to the varnished corridor, where there was a pay phone. He liked dialling, but out of long discipline never did without a reason.

Soon after Christmas Mme. Carette came to see him, wearing Berthe's velvet boots with tassels, Berthe's dyed rabbit coat, and a feather turban of her own. Instead of praying for guidance Marie had fallen in love with one of the Greeks who were starting to move into their part of Montreal. There had never been a foreigner in the family, let alone a pagan. Her uncle interrupted to remark that Greeks were usually Christians, though of the wrong kind for Marie. Mme. Carette implored him to find someone, not a Greek, of the right kind: sober, established, Catholic, French-speaking, natively Canadian. "Not Canadian from New England," she said, showing a brief ingratitude to Fall River. She left a store of nickels, so that he could ring her whenever he liked.

Louis Driscoll, French in all but name, called on Marie for the first time on the twelfth of April 1950. Patches of dirty snow still lay against the curb. The trees on Rue Saint-Hubert looked dark and brittle, as though winter had killed them at last. From behind the parlor curtain, unseen from the street, the Carette women watched him coming along from the bus stop. To meet Marie he had put on a beige tweed overcoat, loosely belted, a beige scarf, a bottle-green snap-brim fedora, crêpe-soled shoes, pigskin gloves. His trousers were sharply pressed, a shade darker than the hat. Under his left arm he held close a parcel in white paper, the size and shape of a two-pound box of Laura Secord chocolates. He stopped frequently to consult the house numbers (blue-and-white, set rather high, Montreal style), which he compared with a slip of paper brought close to his eyes.

It was too bad that he had to wear glasses; the Carettes were not prepared for that, or for the fringe of ginger hair below his hat. Uncle Gildas had said he was of distinguished appearance. He came from Moncton, New Brunswick, and was employed at the head office of a pulp-and-paper concern. His age was twenty-six. Berthe thought that he must be a failed seminarist; they were the only Catholic bachelors Uncle Gildas knew.

Peering at their front door, he walked into a puddle of slush. Mme. Carette wondered if Marie's children were going to be nearsighted. "How can we be sure he's the right man?" she said.

"Who else could he be?" Berthe replied. What did he want with Marie? Uncle Gildas could not have promised much in her name, apart from a pliant nature. There could never be a meeting in a notary's office to discuss a dowry, unless you counted some plates and furniture. The old man may have frightened Louis, reminded him that prolonged celibacy—except among the clergy—is displeasing to God. Marie is poor, he must have said, though honorably connected. She will feel grateful to you all her life.

Their front steps were painted pearl-gray, to match the building stone. Louis's face, upturned, was the color of wood ash. Climbing the stair, ringing the front doorbell could change his life in a way he did not wholly desire. Probably he wanted a woman without sin or risk or coaxing or remorse; but did he want her enough to warrant setting up a household? A man with a memory as transient as his, who could read an address thirty times and still let it drift, might forget to come to the wedding. He crumpled the slip of paper, pushed it inside a tweed pocket, withdrew a large handkerchief, blew his nose.

Mme. Carette swayed back from the curtain as though a stone had been flung. She concluded some private thought by addressing Marie: ". . . although I will feel better on my deathbed if I

**16**

know you are in your own home." Louis meanwhile kicked the bottom step, getting rid of snow stuck to his shoes. (Rustics kicked and stamped. Marie's Greek had wiped his feet.) Still he hesitated, sliding a last pale look in the direction of buses and streetcars. Then, as he might have turned a gun on himself, he climbed five steps and pressed his finger to the bell.

"Somebody has to let him in," said Mme. Carette.

"Marie," said Berthe.

"It wouldn't seem right. She's never met him."

He stood quite near, where the top step broadened to a small platform level with the window. They could have leaned out, introduced him to Marie. Marie at this moment seemed to think he would do; at least, she showed no sign of distaste, such as pushing out her lower lip or crumpling her chin. Perhaps she had been getting ready to drop her Greek: Mme. Carette had warned her that she would have to be a servant to his mother, and eat peculiar food. "He's never asked me to," said Marie, and that was part of the trouble. He hadn't asked anything. For her twenty-first birthday he had given her a locket on a chain and a box from Maitland's, the West End confectioner, containing twenty-one chocolate mice. "He loves me," said Marie. She kept counting the mice and would not let anyone eat them.

In the end it was Berthe who admitted Louis, accepted the gift of chocolates on behalf of Marie, showed him where to leave his hat and coat. She approved of the clean white shirt, the jacket of a tweed similar to the coat but lighter in weight, the tie with a pattern of storm-tossed sailboats. Before shaking hands he removed his glasses, which had misted over, and wiped them dry. His eyes meeting the bright evening at the window (Marie was still there, but with her back to the street) flashed ultramarine. Mme. Carette hoped Marie's children would inherit that color.

He took Marie's yielding hand and let it drop. Freed of the introduction, she pried open the lid of the candy box and said, distinctly, "No mice." He seemed not to hear, or may have thought she was pleased to see he had not played a practical joke. Berthe showed him to the plush armchair, directly underneath a chandelier studded with light bulbs. From this chair Uncle Gildas had explained the whims of God; against its linen antimacassar the Greek had recently rested his head.

Around Louis's crêpe soles pools of snow water formed. Berthe glanced at her mother, meaning that she was not to mind; but Mme. Carette was trying to remember where Berthe had said that she and Marie were to sit. (On the sofa, facing Louis.) Berthe chose a gilt upright chair, from which she could rise easily to pass refreshments. These were laid out on a marble-topped console: vanilla wafers, iced sultana cake, maple fudge, marshmallow biscuits, soft drinks. Behind the sofa a large pier glass reflected Louis in the armchair and the top of Mme. Carette's head. Berthe could tell from her mother's posture, head tilted, hands clasped, that she was silently asking Louis to trust her. She leaned forward and asked him if he was an only child. Berthe closed her eyes. When she opened them, nothing had changed except that Marie was eating chocolates. Louis seemed to be reflecting on his status.

He was the oldest of seven, he finally said. The others were Joseph, Raymond, Vincent, Francis, Rose, and Claire. French was their first language, in a way. But, then, so was English. A certain Louis Joseph Raymond Driscoll, Irish, veteran of Waterloo on the decent side, proscribed in England and Ireland as a result, had come out to Canada and grafted on pure French stock a number of noble traits: bright, wavy hair, a talent for public speaking, another for social aplomb. In every generation of Driscolls, there had to be a Louis, a Joseph, a Raymond. (Berthe and her mother exchanged a look. He wanted three sons.)

His French was slow and muffled, as though strained through wool. He used English words, or French words in an English way. Mme. Carette lifted her shoulders and parted her clasped hands as if to say, Never mind, English is better than Greek. At least, they could be certain that the Driscolls were Catholic. In

August his father and mother were making the Holy Year pilgrimage to Rome.

Rome was beyond their imagining, though all three Carettes had been to Maine and Old Orchard Beach. Louis hoped to spend a vacation in Old Orchard (in response to an ardent question from Mme. Carette), but he had more feeling for Quebec City. His father's people had entered Canada by way of Quebec.

"The French part of the family?" said Mme. Carette.

"Yes, yes," said Berthe, touching her mother's arm.

Berthe had been to Quebec City, said Mme. Carette. She was brilliant, reliable, fully bilingual. Her office promoted her every January. They were always sending her away on company business. She knew Plattsburgh, Saranac Lake. In Quebec City, at lunch at the Château Frontenac, she had seen well-known politicians stuffing down oysters and fresh lobster, at taxpayers' expense.

Louis's glance tried to cross Berthe's, as he might have sought out and welcomed a second man in the room. Berthe reached past Mme. Carette to take the candy box away from Marie. She nudged her mother with her elbow.

"The first time I ever saw Old Orchard," Mme. Carette resumed, smoothing the bodice of her dress, "I was sorry I had not gone there on my honeymoon." She paused, watching Louis accept a chocolate. "My husband and I went to Fall River. He had a brother in the lumber business."

At the mention of lumber, Louis took on a set, bulldog look. Berthe wondered if the pulp-and-paper firm had gone bankrupt. Her thoughts rushed to Uncle Gildas—how she would have it out with him, not leave it to her mother, if he had failed to examine Louis's prospects. But then Louis began to cough and had to cover his mouth. He was in trouble with a caramel. The Carettes looked away, so that he could strangle unobserved. "How dark it is," said Berthe, to let him think he could not be

**19**

seen. Marie got up, with a hiss and rustle of taffeta skirt, and switched on the twin floor lamps with their cerise silk shades.

There, she seemed to be saying to Berthe. Have I done the right thing? Is this what you wanted?

Louis still coughed, but weakly. He moved his fingers, like a child made to wave goodbye. Mme. Carette wondered how many contagious children's diseases he had survived; in a large family everything made the rounds. His eyes, perhaps seeking shade, moved across the brown wallpaper flecked with gold and stopped at the only familiar sight in the room—his reflection in the pier glass. He sat up straighter and quite definitely swallowed. He took a long drink of ginger ale. "When Irish eyes are smiling," he said, in English, as if to himself. "When Irish eyes are smiling. There's a lot to be said for that. A lot to be said."

Of course he was at a loss, astray in an armchair, with the Carettes watching like friendly judges. When he reached for another chocolate, they looked to see if his nails were clean. When he crossed his legs, they examined his socks. They were fixing their first impression of the stranger who might take Marie away, give her a modern kitchen, children to bring up, a muskrat coat, a charge account at Dupuis Frères department store, a holiday in Maine. Louis continued to examine his bright Driscoll hair, the small nose along which his glasses slid. Holding the glasses in place with a finger, he answered Mme. Carette: His father was a dental surgeon, with a degree from Pennsylvania. It was the only degree worth mentioning. Before settling into a dentist's chair the patient should always read the writing on the wall. His mother was born Lucarne, a big name in Moncton. She could still get into her wedding dress. Everything was so conveniently arranged at home—cavernous washing machine, giant vacuum cleaner—that she seldom went out. When she did, she wore a two-strand cultured-pearl necklace and a coat and hat of Persian lamb.

The Carettes could not match this, though they were related to families for whom bridges were named. Mme. Carette sat on the edge of the sofa, ankles together. Gentility was the brace that kept her upright. She had once been a young widow, hard pressed, had needed to sew for money. Berthe recalled a stricter, an unsmiling mother, straining over pleats and tucks for clients who reneged on pennies. She wore the neutral shades of half-mourning, the whitish grays of Rue Saint-Hubert, as though everything had to be used up—even remnants of grief.

Mme. Carette tried to imagine Louis's mother. She might one day have to sell the pearls; even a dentist trained in Pennsylvania could leave behind disorder and debts. Whatever happened, she said to Louis, she would remain in this flat. Even after the girls were married. She would rather beg on the steps of the parish church than intrude upon a young marriage. When her last, dreadful illness made itself known, she would creep away to the Hôtel Dieu and die without a murmur. On the other hand, the street seemed to be filling up with foreigners. She might have to move.

Berthe and Marie were dressed alike, as if to confound Louis, force him to choose the true princess. Leaving the sight of his face in the mirror, puzzled by death and old age, he took notice of the two moiré skirts, organdie blouses, patent-leather belts. "I can't get over those twins of yours," he said to Mme. Carette. "I just can't get over them."

Once, Berthe had tried Marie in her own office—easy work, taking messages when the switchboard was closed. She knew just enough English for that. After two weeks the office manager, Mr. Macfarlane, had said to Berthe, "Your sister is an angel, but angels aren't in demand at Prestige Central Burners."

It was the combination of fair hair and dark eyes, the enchanting misalliance, that gave Marie the look of an angel. She played with the locket the Greek had given her, twisting and unwinding the chain. What did she owe her Greek? Fidelity? An explanation? He was punctual and polite, had never laid a hand on her, in temper or eagerness, had travelled a long way by streetcar to bring back the mice. True, said Berthe, reviewing his good points, while Louis ate the last of the fudge. It was true about the mice, but he should have become more than "Marie's Greek." In the life of a penniless unmarried young woman, there was no room for a man merely in love. He ought to have presented himself as *something*: Marie's future.

In May true spring came, moist and hot. Berthe brought home new dress patterns and yards of flowered rayon and piqué. Louis called three evenings a week, at seven o'clock, after the supper dishes were cleared away. They played hearts in the dining room, drank Salada tea, brewed black, with plenty of sugar and cream, ate éclairs and mille-feuilles from Celentano, the bakery on Avenue Mont Royal. (Celentano had been called something else for years now, but Mme. Carette did not take notice of change of that kind, and did not care to have it pointed out.) Louis, eating coffee éclairs one after another, told stories set in Moncton that showed off his family. Marie wore a blue dress with a red collar, once Berthe's, and a red barrette in her hair. Berthe, a master player, held back to let Louis win. Mme. Carette listened to Louis, kept some of his stories, discarded others, garnering information useful to Marie. Marie picked up cards at random, disrupting the game. Louis's French was not as woolly as before, but he had somewhere acquired a common Montreal accent. Mme. Carette wondered who his friends were and how Marie's children would sound.

They began to invite him to meals. He arrived at half past five, straight from work, and was served at once. Mme. Carette told Berthe that she hoped he washed his hands at the office, because he never did here. They used the blue-willow-pattern china that would go to Marie. One evening, when the tablecloth had been folded and put away, and the teacups and cards distributed, he mentioned marriage—not his own, or to anyone in particular, but as a way of life. Mme. Carette broke in to say that she had been widowed at Louis's age. She recalled what it had been like

22

to have a husband she could consult and admire. "Marriage means children," she said, looking fondly at her own. She would not be alone during her long, final illness. The girls would take her in. She would not be a burden; a couch would do for a bed.

Louis said he was tired of the game. He dropped his hand and spread the cards in an arc.

"So many hearts," said Mme. Carette, admiringly.

"Let me see." Marie had to stand: there was a large teapot in the way. "Ace, queen, ten, eight, five . . . a wedding." Before Berthe's foot reached her ankle, she managed to ask, sincerely, if anyone close to him was getting married this year.

Mme. Carette considered Marie as good as engaged. She bought a quantity of embroidery floss and began the ornamentation of guest towels and tea towels, place mats and pillow slips. Marie ran her finger over the pretty monogram with its intricate frill of vine leaves. Her mind, which had sunk into hibernation when she accepted Louis and forgot her Greek, awoke and plagued her with a nightmare. "I became a nun" was all she told her mother. Mme. Carette wished it were true. Actually, the dream had stopped short of vows. Barefoot, naked under a robe of coarse brown wool, she moved along an aisle in and out of squares of sunlight. At the altar they were waiting to shear her hair. A strange man—not Uncle Gildas, not Louis, not the Greek—got up out of a pew and stood barring her way. The rough gown turned out to be frail protection. All that kept the dream from sliding into blasphemy and abomination was Marie's entire unacquaintance, awake or asleep, with what could happen next.

Because Marie did not like to be alone in the dark, she and Berthe still shared a room. Their childhood bed had been taken away and supplanted by twin beds with quilted satin headboards. Berthe had to sleep on three pillows, because the aluminum hair curlers she wore ground into her scalp. First thing every morning, she clipped on her pearl earrings, sat up, and unwound the curlers, which she handed one by one to Marie.

23

Marie put her own hair up and kept it that way until suppertime.

In the dark, her face turned to the heap of pillows dimly seen, Marie told Berthe about the incident in the chapel. If dreams are life's opposite, what did it mean? Berthe saw that there was more to it than Marie was able to say. Speaking softly, so that their mother would not hear, she tried to tell Marie about men—what they were like and what they wanted. Marie suggested that she and Berthe enter a cloistered convent together, now, while there was still time. Berthe supposed that she had in mind the famous Martin sisters of Lisieux, in France, most of them Carmelites and one a saint. She touched her own temple, meaning that Marie had gone soft in the brain. Marie did not see; if she had, she would have thought that Berthe was easing a curler. Berthe reminded Marie that she was marked out not for sainthood in France but for marriage in Montreal. Berthe had a salary and occasional travel. Mme. Carette had her Fall River bounty. Marie, if she put her mind to it, could have a lifetime of love.

"Is Louis love?" said Marie.

There were girls ready to line up in the rain for Louis, said Berthe.

"What girls?" said Marie, perplexed rather than disbelieving.

"Montreal girls," said Berthe. "The girls who cry with envy when you and Louis walk down the street."

"We have never walked down a street," said Marie.


The third of June was Louis's birthday. He arrived wearing a new seersucker suit. The Carettes offered three monogrammed hem-stitched handkerchiefs—he was always polishing his glasses or mopping his face. Mme. Carette had prepared a meal he particularly favored—roast pork and coconut layer cake. The sun was still high. His birthday unwound in a steady, blazing afternoon. He suddenly put his knife and fork down and said that if he ever decided to get married he would need more than his annual bonus to pay for the honeymoon. He would have to buy carpets, lamps, a refrigerator. People talked lightly of marriage without considering the cost for the groom. Priests urged the married condition on bachelors—priests, who did not know the price of eight ounces of tea.

"Some brides bring lamps and lampshades," said Mme. Carette. "A glass-front bookcase. Even the books to put in it." Her husband had owned a furniture shop on Rue Saint-Denis. Household goods earmarked for Berthe and Marie had been stored with relatives for some twenty years, waxed and polished and free of dust. "An oak table that seats fourteen," she said, and stopped with that. Berthe had forbidden her to draw up an inventory. They were not bartering Marie.

"Some girls have money," said Marie. Her savings—eighteen dollars—were in a drawer of her mother's old treadle sewing machine.

A spasm crossed Louis's face; he often choked on his food. Berthe knew more about men than Marie—more than her mother, who knew only how children come about. Mr. Ryder, of Berthe's office, would stand in the corridor, letting elevators go by, waiting for a chance to squeeze in next to Berthe. Mr. Sexton had offered her money, a regular allowance, if she would go out with him every Friday, the night of his Legion meeting. Mr. Macfarlane had left a lewd poem on her desk, then a note of apology, then a poem even worse than the first. Mr. Wright-Ashburton had offered to leave his wife—for, of course, they had wives, Mr. Ryder, Mr. Sexton, Mr. Macfarlane, none of whom she had ever encouraged, and Mr. Wright-Ashburton, with whom she had been to Plattsburgh and Saranac Lake, and whose private behavior she had described, kneeling, in remote parishes, where the confessor could not have known her by voice.

When Berthe accepted Mr. Wright-Ashburton's raving proposal to leave his wife, saying that Irene probably knew about them anyway, would be thankful to have it in the clear, his face had wavered with fright, like a face seen underwater—rippling, uncontrolled. Berthe had to tell him she hadn't meant it. She could not marry a divorced man. On Louis's face she saw that same quivering dismay. He was afraid of Marie, of her docility, her monogrammed towels, her dependence, her glass-front bookcase. Having seen this, Berthe was not surprised when he gave no further sign of life until the twenty-fifth of June.

During his absence the guilt and darkness of rejection filled every corner of the flat. There was not a room that did not speak of humiliation—oh, not because Louis had dropped Marie but because the Carettes had honored and welcomed a clodhopper, a cheapjack, a ginger-haired nobody. Mme. Carette and Marie made many telephone calls to his office, with a variety of names and voices, to be told every time he was not at his desk. One morning Berthe, on her way to work, saw someone very like him hurrying into Windsor Station. By the time she had struggled out of her crowded streetcar, he was gone. She followed him into the great concourse and looked at the times of the different trains and saw where they were going. A trapped sparrow fluttered under the glass roof. She recalled an expression of Louis's, un-easy and roguish, when he had told Berthe that Marie did not understand the facts of life. (This in English, over the table, as if Mme. Carette and Marie could not follow.) When Berthe asked what these facts might be, he had tried to cross her glance, as on that first evening, one man to another. She was not a man; she had looked away.


Mme. Carette went on embroidering baskets of flowers, ivy leaves, hunched over her work, head down. Marie decided to find a job as a receptionist in a beauty salon. It would be pleasant work in clean surroundings. A girl she had talked to on the bus earned fourteen dollars a week. Marie would give her mother eight and keep six. She did not need Louis, she said, and she was sure she could never love him.

"No one expected you to love him," said her mother, without looking up.

On the morning of the twenty-fifth of June he rang the front doorbell. Marie was eating breakfast in the kitchen, wearing Berthe's aluminum curlers under a mauve chiffon scarf, and Berthe's mauve-and-black kimono. He stood in the middle of the room, refusing offers of tea, and said that the whole world was engulfed in war. Marie looked out the kitchen window, at bare yards and storage sheds.

"Not there," said Louis. "In Korea."

Marie and her mother had never heard of the place. Mme. Carette took it for granted that the British had started something again. She said, "They can't take you, Louis, because of your eyesight." Louis replied that this time they would take everybody, bachelors first. A few married men might be allowed to make themselves useful at home. Mme. Carette put her arms around him. "You are my son now," she said. "I'll never let them ship you to England. You can hide in our coal shed." Marie had not understood that the mention of war was a marriage proposal, but her mother had grasped it at once. She wanted to call Berthe and tell her to come home immediately, but Louis was in a hurry to publish the banns. Marie retired to the bedroom and changed into Berthe's white sharkskin sundress and jacket and toeless white suède shoes. She smoothed Berthe's suntan makeup on her legs, hoping that her mother would not see she was not wearing stockings. She combed out her hair, put on lipstick and earrings, and butterfly sunglasses belonging to Berthe. Then, for the first time, she and Louis together walked down the front steps to the street.

At Marie's parish church they found other couples standing about, waiting for advice. They had heard the news and decided to get married at once. Marie and Louis held hands, as though they had been engaged for a long time. She hoped no one would notice that she had no engagement ring. Unfortunately, their banns could not be posted until July, or the marriage take place until August. His parents would not be present to bless them: at the very day and hour of the ceremony they would be on their way to Rome.

The next day, Louis went to a jeweller on Rue Saint-Denis, recommended by Mme. Carette, but he was out of engagement rings. He had sold every last one that day. Louis did not look anywhere else; Mme. Carette had said he was the only man she trusted. Louis's mother sent rings by registered mail. They had been taken from the hand of her dead sister, who had wanted them passed on to her son, but the son had vanished into Springfield and no longer sent Christmas cards. Mme. Carette shook her own wedding dress out of tissue paper and made a few adjustments so that it would fit Marie. Since the war it had become impossible to find silk of that quality.

Waiting for August, Louis called on Marie every day. They rode the streetcar up to Avenue Mont Royal to eat barbecued chicken. (One evening Marie let her engagement ring fall into a crack of the corrugated floor of the tram, and a number of strangers told her to be careful, or she would lose her man, too.) The chicken arrived on a bed of chips, in a wicker basket. Louis showed Marie how to eat barbecue without a knife and fork. Fortunately, Mme. Carette was not there to watch Marie gnawing on a bone. She was sewing the rest of the trousseau and had no time to act as chaperon.

Berthe's office sent her to Buffalo for a long weekend. She brought back match folders from Polish and German restaurants, an ashtray on which was written "Buffalo Hofbrau," and a number of articles that were much cheaper down there, such as nylon stockings. Marie asked if they still ate with knives and forks in Buffalo, or if they had caught up to Montreal. Alone together, Mme. Carette and Berthe sat in the kitchen and gossiped about Louis. The white summer curtains were up; the coal-and-wood range was covered with clean white oilcloth. Berthe had a new kimono—white, with red pagodas on the sleeves. She propped her new red mules on the oven door. She smoked now, and carried everywhere the Buffalo Hofbrau ashtray. Mme. Carette made Berthe promise not to smoke in front of Uncle Gildas, or in the street, or at Marie's wedding reception, or in the front parlor, where the smell might get into the curtains. Sometimes they had just tea and toast and Celentano pastry for supper. When Berthe ate a coffee éclair, she said, "Here's one Louis won't get."

The bright evenings of suppers and card games slid into the past, and by August seemed long ago. Louis said to Marie, "We knew how to have a good time. People don't enjoy themselves anymore." He believed that the other customers in the barbecue restaurant had secret, nagging troubles. Waiting for the wicker basket of chicken, he held Marie's hand and stared at men who might be Greeks. He tried to tell her what had been on his mind between the third and twenty-fifth of June, but Marie did not care, and he gave up. They came to their first important agreement: neither of them wanted the blue-willow-pattern plates. Louis said he would ask his parents to start them off with six place settings of English Rose. She seemed still to be listening, and so he told her that the name of her parish church, Saint Louis de France, had always seemed to him to be a personal sign of some kind: an obscure force must have guided him to Rue Saint-Hubert and Marie. Her soft brown eyes never wavered. They forgot about Uncle Gildas, and whatever it was Uncle Gildas had said to frighten them.

Louis and Marie were married on the third Saturday of August, with flowers from an earlier wedding banked along the altar rail, and two other wedding parties waiting at the back of the church. Berthe supposed that Marie, by accepting the ring of a dead woman and wearing the gown of another woman widowed at twenty-six, was calling down the blackest kind of misfortune. She remembered her innocent nakedness under the robe of frieze. Marie had no debts. She owed Louis nothing. She had saved him from a long journey to a foreign place, perhaps even from dying. As he placed the unlucky ring on her finger, Berthe wept. She knew that some of the people looking on—Uncle

Gildas, or Joseph and Raymond Driscoll, amazing in their ginger likeness—were mistaking her for a jealous older sister, longing to be in Marie's place.

Marie, now Mme. Driscoll, turned to Berthe and smiled, as she used to when they were children. Once again, the smile said, Have I done the right thing? Is this what you wanted? Yes, yes, said Berthe silently, but she went on crying. Marie had always turned to Berthe; she had started to walk because she wanted to be with Berthe. She had been standing, holding on to a kitchen chair, and she suddenly smiled and let go. Later, when Marie was three, and in the habit of taking her clothes off and showing what must never be seen, Mme. Carette locked her into the storage shed behind the kitchen. Berthe knelt on her side of the door, sobbing, calling, "Don't be afraid, Marie. Berthe is here." Mme. Carette relented and unlocked the door, and there was Marie, wearing just her undershirt, smiling for Berthe.

Leading her mother, Berthe approached the altar rail. Marie seemed contented; for Berthe, that was good enough. She kissed her sister, and kissed the chosen husband. He had not separated them but would be a long incident in their lives. Among the pictures that were taken on the church steps, there is one of Louis with an arm around each sister and the sisters trying to clasp hands behind his back.

The wedding party walked in a procession down the steps and around the corner: another impression in black-and-white. The August pavement burned under the women's thin soles. Their fine clothes were too hot. Children playing in the road broke into applause when they saw Marie. She waved her left hand, showing the ring. The children were still French-Canadian; so were the neighbors, out on their balconies to look at Marie. Three yellow leaves fell—white, in a photograph. One of the Driscoll boys raced ahead and brought the party to a stop. There is Marie, who does not yet understand that she is leaving home, and confident Louis, so soon to have knowledge of her bewildering ignorance.

## The Chosen Husband

Berthe saw the street as if she were bent over the box camera, trying to keep the frame straight. It was an important picture, like a precise instrument of measurement: so much duty, so much love, so much reckless safety—the distance between last April and now. She thought, It had to be done. They began to walk again. Mme. Carette realized for the first time what she and Uncle Gildas and Berthe had brought about: the unredeemable loss of Marie. She said to Berthe, "Wait until I am dead before you get married. You can marry a widower. They make good husbands." Berthe was nearly twenty-four, just at the limit. She had turned away so many attractive prospects, with no explanation, and had frightened so many others with her skill at cards and her quick blue eyes that word had spread, and she was not solicited as before.

Berthe and Marie slipped away from the reception—moved, that is, from the parlor to the bedroom—so that Berthe could help her sister pack. It turned out that Mme. Carette had done the packing. Marie had never had to fill a suitcase, and would not have known what to put in first. For a time, they sat on the edge of a bed, talking in whispers. Berthe smoked, holding the Buffalo Hofbrau ashtray. She showed Marie a black lacquer cigarette lighter she had not shown her mother. Marie had started to change her clothes; she was just in her slip. She looked at the lighter on all sides and handed it back. Louis was taking her to the Château Frontenac, in Quebec City, for three nights—the equivalent of ten days in Old Orchard, he had said. After that, they would go straight to the duplex property, quite far north on Boulevard Pie IX, that his father was helping him buy. "I'll call you tomorrow morning," said Marie, for whom tomorrow was still the same thing as today. If Uncle Gildas had been at Berthe's mercy, she would have held his head underwater. Then she thought, Why blame him? She and Marie were Montreal girls, not trained to accompany heroes, or to hold out for dreams, but just to be patient.

31

# From Cloud to Cloud

The family's experience of Raymond was like a long railway journey with a constantly shifting point of view. His mother and aunt were of a generation for whom travel had meant trains—slow trips there and back, with an intense engagement in eating, or a game of cards with strangers, interrupted by a flash of celestial light from the frozen and sunstruck St. Lawrence. Then came the dark-brown slums of the approach to Montreal, the signal to get one's luggage down from the rack.

To make a short story shorter, his Aunt Berthe (she worked in an office full of English-Canadians) would have said Raymond was Heaven and Hell. Mother and aunt, the two sisters had thought they never could love anymone more than Raymond; then, all at once, he seemed to his aunt so steadily imperfect, so rigid in his failings, that the changing prospect of his moods, decisions, needs, life ceased to draw her attention.

He'd had a father, of course—had him until he was eighteen, even though it was Raymond's practice to grumble that he had been raised, badly, by women. His last memories of his father must surely have been Louis dying of emphysema, upright in the white-painted wicker chair, in blazing forbidden sunlight, mangling a forbidden cigar. The partially flagged backyard had no shade in it—just two yellow fringed umbrellas that filtered the blue of July and made it bilious. Louis could not sit in their bogus shadow, said it made him sweat. Behind the umbrellas was the kitchen entrance to a duplex dwelling of stucco and brick, late 1940s in style—a cube with varnished doors—at the northern end of Boulevard Pie IX. "Remember that your father owned his own home," said Louis; also, "When we first moved up here, you could still see vacant lots. It depressed your mother. She wasn't used to an open view."

Where Raymond's sandbox had been stood a granite birdbath with three aluminum birds the size of pigeons perched on the rim—the gift from Louis's firm when he had to take early retirement, because he was so ill. He already owned a gold watch. He told Raymond exactly where to find the watch in his desk—in which drawer. Raymond sat cross-legged on the grass and practiced flipping a vegetable knife; his mother had found and disposed of his commando dagger. His father could draw breath but had to pause before he spoke. Waiting for strength, he looked up at the sky, at a moon in sunlight, pale and transparent—a memory of dozens of other waning moons. (It was the summer of the moon walk. Raymond's mother still mentions this, as though it had exerted a tidal influence on her affairs.)

The silent intermissions, his gaze upturned, made it seem as if Louis were seeking divine assistance. Actually, he knew everything he wished to say. So did Raymond. Raymond—even his aunt will not deny it—showed respect. He never once remarked, "I've heard this before," or uttered the timeless, frantic snub of the young, "I know, I know, I *know*."

His father said, "There have always been good jobs in Boston," "Never forget your French, because it would break your mother's heart," "One of these days you're going to have to cut your hair," "Marry a Catholic, but not just any Catholic," "With a name like Raymond Joseph Driscoll you can go any- where in the world," "That autograph album of mine is worth a fortune. Hang on to it. It will always get you out of a tight spot."

In his lifetime Louis wrote to hockey players and film stars and local politicians, and quite often received an answer. Ray- mond as a child watched him cutting out the signature and pasting it in a deep-blue leather-bound book. Now that Ray- mond is settled in Florida, trying to build a career in the motel business, his whole life is a tight spot. He finds it hard to credit that the album is worth nothing. Unfortunately, it is so. Most of the signatures were facsimiles, or had been dashed off by a secre- tary. The few authentic autographs were of names too obscure to matter. The half dozen that Louis purchased from a special- ized dealer on Peel Street, since driven out of business, were certified fakes. Louis kept "Joseph Stalin" and "Harry S Tru- man" in a locked drawer, telling Marie, his wife, that if Canada was ever occupied by one of the two great powers, or by both at once, she would be able to barter her way to safety.

Raymond had a thin mane of russet hair that covered his profile when he bent over to retrieve the knife. He wore circus- rodeo gear, silver and white. Louis couldn't stand the sight of his son's clothes; in his dying crankiness he gave some away. Ray- mond stored his favorite outfits at his aunt's place. She lived in a second-story walkup, with front and back balconies, a long, cool hall, three bedrooms, on the west side of Parc Lafontaine. She was unmarried and did not need all that space; she enjoyed just walking from room to room. Louis spoke to Raymond in English, so that he would be able to make his way in the world. He wanted him to go to an English commercial school, where he might meet people who would be useful to him later on. Ray- mond's aunt said that her English was better than Louis's: his "th" sometimes slipped into "d." Louis, panting, mentioned to Raymond that Berthe, for all her pretensions, was not as well off propertywise as her sister and brother-in-law, though she seemed to have more money to throw around. "Low rent in any crummy neighborhood—that's her creed," said Raymond's father. In his last, bad, bitter days, he seemed to be brooding over Berthe, compared her career with his own, said she had an inborn craving for sleeping with married men. But before he died he took every word back, said she had been a good friend to him, was an example for other women, though not necessarily married women. He wanted her to keep an eye on Marie and Raymond—he said he felt as if he were leaving behind two helpless children, one eighteen, the other in her forties, along with the two cars, the valuable autograph album, the gold watch, and the paid-up house.

Louis also left a handwritten inconvenient request to be buried in New Brunswick, where he came from, rather than in Montreal. Raymond's mother hid the message behind a sofa cushion, where it would be discovered during some future heavy cleaning. She could not bring herself to tear it up. They buried Louis in Notre Dame des Neiges cemetery, where Marie intended to join him, not too soon. She ordered a bilingual inscription on the gravestone, because he had spoken English at the office and French to her.

Raymond in those days spoke French and English, too, with a crack in each. His English belonged to a subdivision of Catholic Montreal—a bit Irish-sounding but thinner than any tone you might hear in Dublin. His French vocabulary was drawn from conversations with his mother and aunt, and should have been full of tenderness. He did not know what he wanted to be. "If I ever write, I'm going to write a book about the family," he told his aunt the day of Louis's funeral, looking at the relatives in their black unnatural clothes, soaking up heat. It was the first time he had ever said this, and most likely the last. Poor Raymond could barely scrawl a letter, couldn't spell. He didn't mind learning, but he hated to be taught. After he left home, Berthe and Marie scarcely had the sight of his handwriting. They had his voice over the telephone, calling from different American places (they thought of Vietnam as an American place) with a gradually altered accent. His French filled up with English, as with a deposit of pebbles and sand, and in English he became not quite a stranger: even years later he still said "palm" to rhyme with "jam."

Raymond behaved correctly at the funeral, holding his mother's arm, seeing that everyone had a word with her, causing those relatives who did not know him well to remark that he was his father all over again. He was dressed in a dark suit, bought in a hurry, and one of Louis's ties. He had not worn a tie since the last family funeral; Berthe had to fasten the knot. He let her give his hair a light trim, so that it cleared his shoulders.

Marie would not hold a reception: the mourners had to settle for a kiss or a handshake beside the open grave. Louis's people, some of whom had come a long way, were starting back with the pieces of a break beyond mending. Marie didn't care: her family feelings had narrowed to Raymond and Berthe. After the funeral, Raymond drove the two sisters to Berthe's flat. He sat with his mother at the kitchen table and watched Berthe cutting up a cold chicken. Marie kept on her funeral hat, a black straw pillbox with a wisp of veil. No one said much. The chicken was not enough for Raymond, so Berthe got out the ham she had baked the night before in case Marie changed her mind about inviting the relatives. She put the whole thing down in front of him, and he hacked pieces off and ate with his fingers. Marie said, "You wouldn't dare do that if your father could see you," because she had to say something. She and Berthe knew he was having a bad time.

When he finished, they moved down the hall to Berthe's living room. She opened the doors to both balconies, to invite a cross breeze. The heated air touched the looped white curtain without stirring a fold of it. Raymond took off his jacket and tie. The women had already removed their black stockings. Respect for Louis kept them from making themselves entirely comfortable. They had nothing in particular to do for the rest of the day. Berthe had taken time off from the office, and Marie was afraid to go home. She believed that some essence of Louis, not quite a ghost, was in their house on Boulevard Pie IX, testing locks, turning door handles, sliding drawers open, handling Marie's poor muddled household accounts, ascertaining once and for all the exact amount of money owed by Marie to Berthe. (Berthe had always been good for a small loan toward the end of the month. She had shown Marie how to entangle the books, so that Louis need never know.)

Raymond stretched out on Berthe's pale-green sofa, with a pile of cushions under his head. "Raymond, watch where you put your feet," said his mother.

"It doesn't matter," said Berthe. "Not today."

"I don't want you to wish we weren't here," said Marie. "After we've moved in, I mean. You'll never know we're in the house. Raymond, ask Aunt Berthe for an ashtray."

"There's one right beside him," said Berthe.

"I won't let Raymond put his feet all over the furniture," said Marie. "Not after today. If you don't want us, all you have to do is say."

"I have said," said Berthe, at which Raymond turned his head and looked at her intently.

Tears flooded Marie's eyes at the improbable vision of Berthe ordering her nearest relatives, newly bereaved, to pack and go. "We're going to be happy, because we love each other," she said.

"Have you asked Raymond where he wants to live?" said Berthe.

"Raymond wants whatever his mother wants," said Marie. "He'll be nice. I promise. He'll take the garbage down. Won't you, Raymond? You'll take the garbage out every night for Aunt Berthe?"

"Not every night," said his aunt. "Twice a week. Don't cry. Louis wouldn't want to see you in tears."

A quiver of shyness touched all three. Louis returned to memory in superior guise, bringing guidance, advice. "Papa wouldn't mind if we watched the news," said Raymond.

For less than a minute they stared at a swaying carpet of jungle green, filmed from a helicopter, and heard a French voice with a Montreal accent describe events in a place the sisters intended never to visit. Raymond jumped to an English channel, without asking if anyone minded. He was the male head of the family now; in any case, they had always given in. Vietnam in English appeared firmly grounded, with a Canadian sergeant in the Marine Corps—shorn, cropped, gray-eyed, at ease. He spoke to Raymond, saying that it was all right for a Canadian to enlist in a foreign army.

"Who cares?" said Marie, fatally. English on television always put her to sleep. She leaned back in her armchair and began very gently to snore. Berthe removed Marie's glasses and her hat, and covered her bare legs with a lace quilt. Even in the warmest weather she could wake up feeling chilled and unloved. She fainted easily; it was her understanding that the blood in her arms and legs congealed, leaving her brain unattended. She seemed content with this explanation and did not seek another.

Raymond sat up, knocking over the pile of cushions. He gathered his hair into a topknot and held it fast. "They send you to San Diego," he said. What was he seeing, really? Pacific surf? A parade in sunlight? Berthe should have asked.

When Marie came to, yawning and sighing, Berthe was putting color on her nails (she had removed it for the funeral) and Raymond was eating chocolate cake, watching Rod Laver. He had taken off his shirt, shoes, and socks. "Laver's the greatest man in the modern world," he said.

"Ah, Raymond," said his mother. "You've already forgotten your father."

As Marie had promised, he carried the garbage out, making a

good impression on the Portuguese family who lived downstairs. (Louis, who would not speak to strangers, had made no impression at all.) At five o'clock the next morning, Berthe's neighbor, up because he had an early delivery at his fruit store, saw Raymond throw a duffel kit into his mother's car and drive away. His hair was tied back with a white leather thong. He wore one of his rodeo outfits and a pair of white boots.

Before leaving Berthe's flat he had rifled her handbag, forgotten on a kitchen chair—a century before, when they assembled for the funeral feast. Before leaving Montreal he made a long detour to say goodbye to his old home. He was not afraid of ghosts, and he had already invented a father who was going to approve of everything he did. In Louis's desk he found the gold watch and one or two documents he knew he would need— among them the birth certificate that showed him eighteen. He took away as a last impression the yellowed grass in the backyard. Nothing had been watered since Louis's death.

Berthe has often wondered what the Marines in the recruiting office down in Plattsburgh made of Raymond, all silver and white, with that lank brick-dust hair and the thin, cracked English. Nothing, probably: they must have expected civilians to resemble fake performers. There was always someone straggling down from Montreal. It was like joining the Foreign Legion. After his first telephone call, Berthe said to Marie, "At least we know where he is," but it was not so; they never quite knew. He did not go to San Diego: a military rule of geography splits the continent. He had enlisted east of the Mississippi, and so he was sent for training to Parris Island. The Canadian Marine had forgotten to mention that possibility. Berthe bought a number of road maps, so that she could look up these new names. The Mississippi seemed to stop dead at Minneapolis. It had nothing to do with Canada. Raymond should have turned the car around and driven home. (Instead, he left it parked in Plattsburgh. He could not remember, later, the name of the street.)

* * *

He has never been back. His excuse used to be that he had nowhere to stay in Montreal. Marie sold the duplex and moved in with Berthe. The last thing he wanted to see on vacation was another standard motel unit, and he knew Berthe wouldn't have him in the house.

He enlisted for four years, then another three. Marie looked upon him as a prisoner, in time to be released. Released honorably? Yes, or he would not have been allowed to settle in Florida: he was still a Canadian in 1976; he could easily have been deported. When he became an American citizen and called Marie, expecting congratulations, she told him that 98 percent of the world's forest fires were started by Americans. It was all she could think of to say. He has been down there ever since, moving like a pendulum between Hollywood North and Hollywood Beach, Fort Lauderdale and the stretch of Miami known as Little Quebec, from the number of French-Canadians who spend holidays there. They have their own newspaper, their own radio station and television channel, they import Montreal barbecue. Hearing their voices sometimes irritates him, sometimes makes him homesick for the summer of 1969, for the ease with which he jumped from cloud to cloud.

Marie still believes that "Parris Island" was one of Raymond's famous spelling mistakes. He must have spent part of his early youth, the least knowable, in a place called Paris, South Carolina. She often wonders about other mothers and sons, and whether children feel any of the pain they inflict. Berthe thinks of how easy it must have been for Raymond to leave, with the sun freshly risen, slanting along side streets, here and there front steps sluiced and dark, the sky not yet a burning glass. He must have supposed the rest of his life was going to be like that. When she and Marie ransacked the house on Boulevard Pie IX, looking for clues, imagining he'd left a letter, left some love, they kept the shades drawn, as if there were another presence in the rooms, tired of daylight.

# FLORIDA

Berthe Carette's sister, Marie, spent eight Christmases of her life in Florida, where her son was establishing a future in the motel industry. Every time Marie went down she found Raymond starting over in a new place: his motels seemed to die on his hands. She used to come back to Montreal riddled with static electricity. Berthe couldn't hand her a teaspoon without receiving a shock, like a small silver bullet. Her sister believed the current was generated by a chemical change that occurred as she flew out of Fort Lauderdale toward a wet, dark, snowy city.

Marie had been living with Berthe ever since 1969, the year her husband died. She still expected what Berthe thought of as husband service: flights met, cabs hailed, doors held, tips attended to. Berthe had to take the bus out to Dorval Airport, with Marie's second-best fur coat over her arm and her high-heeled boots in a plastic bag. Through a glass barrier she could watch her sister gliding through customs, dressed in a new outfit of some sherbet tone—strawberry, lemon-peach—with everything matching, sometimes even her hair. She knew that Marie had been careful to tear the American store and union labels out of the clothes and sew in Canadian ones, in case customs asked her to strip.

"Don't tell me it's still winter," Marie would wail, kissing Berthe as if she had been away for months rather than just a few days. Guiding Marie's arms into the second-best-mink sleeves (paws and piecework), Berthe would get the first of the silvery shocks.

One year, when her son, Raymond, had fallen in love with a divorced woman twice his age (it didn't last), Marie arrived home crackling, exchanging sparks with everything she touched. When she ate a peppermint she felt it detonating in her mouth. Berthe had placed a pot of flowering paper-white narcissi on Marie's dressing table, a welcome-home present reflected on and on in the three mirrors. Marie shuffled along the carpeted passage, still in her boots. She had on her Florida manner, pretending she was in Berthe's flat by mistake. As soon as she saw the plant, she went straight over and gave it a kiss. The flower absorbed a charge and hurled it back. Berthe examined the spot on Marie's lip where the shock had struck. She could find nothing, no trace. Nevertheless Marie applied an ice cube.

She waited until midnight before calling Raymond, to get the benefit of the lower rate. His line was tied up until two: he said the police had been in, investigating a rumor. Marie told about the plant. He made her repeat the story twice, then said she had built up a reserve of static by standing on a shag rug with her boots on. She was not properly grounded when she approached the flower.

"Raymond could have done more with his life," said Marie, hanging up. Berthe, who was still awake, thought he had done all he could, given his brains and character. She did not say so: she never mentioned her nephew, never asked about his health. He had left home young, and caused a lot of grief and trouble.

On Marie's eighth visit, Raymond met her at the airport with a skinny woman he said was his wife. She had dark-blond hair and one of those unset permanents, all corkscrews. Marie looked at her, and looked away. Raymond explained that he had moved back to Hollywood North. Marie said she didn't care, as long as she had somewhere to lay her head.

They left the terminal in silence. Outside, she said, "What's this car? Japanese? Your father liked a Buick."

"It belongs to Mimi," he said.

Marie got in front, next to Raymond, and the skinny woman climbed in behind. Marie said to Raymond, in French, "You haven't told me her name."

"Well, I have, of course. I introduced you. Mimi."

"Mimi isn't a name."

"It's hers," he said.

"It can't be. It's always short for something—for Michèle. Did you ever hear of a Saint Mimi? She's not a divorced woman, is she? You were married in church?"

"In a kind of church," he said. "She belongs to a Christian movement."

Marie knew what that meant: pagan rites. "You haven't joined this thing—this movement?"

"I don't want to join anything," he said. "But it has changed my life."

Marie tried to consider this in an orderly way, going over in her mind the parts of Raymond's life that wanted changing. "What sort of woman would marry an only son without his mother's blessing?" she said.

"Mom," said Raymond, switching to English, and perhaps forgetting she hated to be called this. "She's twenty-nine. I'm thirty-three."

"What's her maiden name?" said Marie.

"Ask her," he said. "I didn't marry her family."

Marie eased the seat belt and turned around, smiling. The woman had her eyes shut. She seemed to be praying. Her skin was freckled, pale for the climate; perhaps she had come to one of the oases of the heart where there are no extremes of weather. As for Raymond, he was sharp and dry, with a high, feverish forehead. His past had evaporated. It annoyed him to have to

speak French. On one of his mother's other visits he had criti-
cized her Montreal accent, said he had heard better French in the
streets of Saigon. He lit a cigarette, but before she could say,
"Your father died of emphysema," threw it out.

Mimi, perhaps made patient by prayer, spoke up: "I am happy
to welcome any mother of Raymond's. May we spend a peaceful
and mutually enriching Christmas." Her voice moved on a
strained, single note, like a soprano recitative. Shyness, Marie
thought. She stole a second look. Her eyes, now open, were pale
blue, with stubby black lashes. She seemed all at once beguiling
and anxious, hoping to be forgiven before having mentioned the
sin. A good point, but not good enough to make her a Catholic.

Raymond carried Marie's luggage to a decent room with
cream walls and tangerine curtains and spread. The motel looked
clean and prosperous, but so had the others. Mimi had gone off
on business of her own. ("I'm feeling sick," she had said, getting
out of the car, with one freckled hand on her stomach and the
other against her throat.)

"She'll be all right," he told Marie.

Alone with Marie, he called her *Maman*, drew her to the
window, showed her a Canadian flag flying next to the Stars and
Stripes. The place was full of Canadians, he said. They stole like
raccoons. One couple had even made off with the bathroom
faucets. "Nice-looking people, too."

"Your father never ran down his own kind," said Marie. She
did not mean to start an argument but to point out certain limits.
He checked the towels, counted the hangers, raised (or lowered,
she could not tell) the air-conditioning. He turned his back while
she changed into her hibiscus-patterned chiffon, in case they
were going out. In a mirror he watched her buckling her red
sandals. Berthe's Christmas present.

"Mimi is the first woman I ever met who reminded me of
you," he said. Marie let that pass. They walked arm in arm
across the parking lot, and he pointed out different things that
might interest her—Quebec license plates, a couple of dying

palms. On the floor of the lobby lay a furled spruce tree, with its branches still tied. Raymond prodded the tree with his running shoe. It had been here for a week, he said, and it was already shedding. Perhaps Marie and Mimi would like to trim it.

"Trim it with what?" said Marie. Every year, for seven years, she had bought decorations, which Raymond had always thrown out with the tree.

"I don't know," he said. "Mimi wants me to set it up on a mirror."

Marie wondered what Raymond's title in this place might be. "Manager," he'd said, but he and Mimi lived like caretakers in an inconvenient arrangement of rooms off the lobby. To get to their kitchen, which was also a storage place for beer and soft drinks, Marie had to squeeze behind the front desk. Every door had a peephole and chain lock. Whenever a bell rang in the lobby Raymond looked carefully before undoing the lock. Another couple worked here, too, he explained, but they were off for Christmas.

The three ate dinner in the kitchen, hemmed in by boxes and crates. Marie asked for an apron, to protect her chiffon. Mimi did not own one, and seemed astonished at the request. She had prepared plain shrimp and boiled rice and plain fruit salad. No wonder Raymond was drying up. Marie showed them pictures of Berthe's Christmas tree, this year red and gold.

Mimi looked for a long time at a snapshot of Berthe, holding a glass, sitting with her legs crossed and her skirt perhaps a bit high. "What's in the glass?" she said.

"Gin does my sister a lot of good," said Marie. She had not enjoyed her shrimp, washed down with some diet drink.

"I'm surprised she never got married," said Mimi. "How old is she? Fifty-something? She still looks good, physically and mentally."

"I am surprised," said Marie, in French. "I am surprised at the turn of this conversation."

"Mimi isn't criticizing Aunt Berthe," said Raymond. "It's a compliment."

Marie turned to Mimi. "My sister never had to get married. She's always made good money. She buys her own fur coats."

Mimi did not know about Berthe, assistant office manager at Prestige Central Burners—a multinational with tentacles in two cities, one of them Cleveland. Last year Mr. Linden from the Cleveland office had invited Berthe out to dinner. His wife had left him; he was getting over the loss. Berthe intended to tell him she had made a lifetime commitment to the firm, with no left-over devotion. She suggested the Ritz-Carlton—she had been there once before, and had a favorite table. During dinner they talked about the different ways of cooking trout, and the bewildering architectural changes taking place in Cleveland and Montreal. Berthe mentioned that whenever a landmark was torn down people said, "It's as bad as Cleveland." It was hard to reconcile the need for progress with the claims of tradition. Mr. Linden said that tradition was flexible.

"I like the way you think," he said. "If only you had been a man, Miss Carette, with your intellect, and your powers of synthesis, you might have gone . . ." and he pointed to the glass bowl of blueberry trifle on the dessert trolley, as if to say, "even farther."

The next day Berthe drew on her retirement savings account and made a down payment on a mink coat (pastel, fully let out) and wore the coat to work. That was her answer. Marie admired this counterstroke more than any feat of history. She wanted Mimi to admire it, too, but she was tired after the flight, and the shock of Raymond's marriage, and the parched, disappointing meal. Halfway through the story her English thinned out.

"What's she saying?" said Mimi. "This man gave her a coat?"

"It's too bad it couldn't have worked out better for Aunt Berthe," said Raymond. "A widower on the executive level. Well, not exactly a widower, but objectively the same thing. Aunt Berthe still looks great. You heard what Mimi said."

"Berthe doesn't need a widower," said Marie. "She can sit on her front balcony and watch widowers running in Parc Lafontaine any Sunday. There's no room in the flat for a widower. All the closets are full. In the spare-room closet there are things belonging to you, Raymond. That beautiful white rodeo belt with the silver buckle Aunt Berthe gave you for your fourteenth birthday. It cost Berthe thirty dollars, in dollars of that time, when the Canadian was worth more than the American."

"Ten cents more," said Raymond.

"Ten cents of another era," said Marie. "Like eighty cents today."

"Aunt Berthe can move if she feels crowded," he said. "Or she can just send me the belt." He spoke to Mimi. "People in Montreal move more often than in any other city in the world. I can show you figures. My father wasn't a Montrealer, so we always lived in just the one house. *Maman* sold it when he died."

"I wouldn't mind seeing that house," said Mimi, as though challenging Marie to produce it.

"Why should Berthe move?" said Marie. "First you want to tie her up with a stranger, then you want to throw her out of her home. She's got a three-bedroom place for a rent you wouldn't believe. She'd be crazy to let it go. It's easier to find a millionaire with clean habits than my sister's kind of flat."

"People don't get married to have three bedrooms," said Mimi, still holding Berthe's picture. "They get married for love and company."

"I am company," said Marie. "I love my sister, and my sister loves me."

"Do you think I married Raymond for *space?*" said Mimi.

Raymond said something in English. Marie did not know what it meant, but it sounded disgusting. "Raymond," she said. "Apologize to your wife."

"Don't talk to him," said Mimi. "You're only working him up."

"Don't you dare knock your chair over," said his mother.

"Raymond! If you go out that door, I won't be here when you get back."

The two women sat quietly after the door slammed. Then Mimi picked up the fallen chair. "That's the real Raymond," she said. "That's Raymond, in public and private. I don't blame any man's mother for the way the man turns out."

"He had hair like wheat," said Marie. "It turned that rusty color when he was three. He had the face of an angel. It's the first time I've ever seen him like this. Of course, he has never been married before."

"He'll be lying on the bed now, sulking," said Mimi. "I'm not used to that. I hadn't been married before, either." She began rinsing plates at the sink. The slit of a window overlooked cars and the stricken palms. Tears ran down her cheeks. She tried to blot them on her arm. "I think he wants to leave me."

"So what if he does leave," said Marie, looking in vain for a clean dish towel. "A bad, disobedient boy. He ran away to Vietnam. The last man in our family. He should have been thinking about having sons instead of travelling around. Raymond's father was called Louis. My father's name was Odilon. Odilon-Louis—that's a nice name for a boy. It goes in any language."

"In my family we just have girls," said Mimi.

"Another thing Raymond did," said Marie. "He stole his father's gold watch. Then he lost it. Just took it and lost it."

"Raymond never lost that watch," said Mimi. "He probably sold it to two or three different people. Raymond will always be Raymond. I'm having a baby. Did he tell you that?"

"He didn't have to," said Marie. "I guessed it when we were in the car. Don't cry anymore. They can hear. The baby can hear you."

He's already heard plenty from Raymond."

Marie's English died. "Look," she said, struggling. "This baby has a grandmother. He's got Berthe. *You've* got Berthe. Never mind Raymond."

"He'll need a father image," said Mimi. "Not just a lot of women."

"Raymond had one," said Marie. "He still joined the Marines."

"He or she," said Mimi. "I don't want to know. I want the surprise. I hope he likes me. She. It feels like a girl."

"It would be good to know in advance," said Marie. "Just for the shopping—to know what to buy. Do you want to save the rest of the shrimp or throw it out?"

"Save it," said Mimi. "Raymond hardly ate anything. He'll be hungry later on."

"That bad boy," said Marie. "I don't care if he never eats again. He'll find out what it's like, alone in the world. Without his mother. Without his aunt. Without his wife. Without his baby."

"I don't want him to be alone," said Mimi, showing Marie her streaked face, the sad little curls stuck to her wet cheeks. "He hasn't actually gone anywhere. I just said I thought he was thinking about it."

Marie tried to remember some of the English Berthe used. When she was talking to people from her office, Berthe would say, "All in good time," and "No way he can do that," and "Count on me," and "Not to worry."

He won't leave you," said Marie. "No way I'll let him do that. Count on me." Her elbow brushed against the handle of the refrigerator door; she felt a silvery spark through the chiffon sleeve. This was the first time such a thing had happened in Florida; it was like an approving message from Berthe. Mimi wiped her hands on a paper towel and turned to Marie.

"Be careful," said Marie, enfolding Raymond's wife and Raymond's baby. "Be careful the baby doesn't get a shock. Everything around here is electric. I'm electric. We'll have to be careful from now on. We've got to make sure we're grounded." She had gone into French, but it didn't matter. The baby could hear, and knew what she meant.

# Dédé

P ascal Brouet is fourteen now. He used to attend a lycée, but after his parents found out about the dealers in the street, outside the gates, they changed him to a private school. Here the situation is about the same, but he hasn't said so; he does not want to be removed again, this time perhaps to a boarding establishment, away from Paris, with nothing decent to eat and lights-out at ten. He would not describe himself as contriving or secretive. He tries to avoid drawing attention to the Responsibility clause in the treaty that governs peace between generations.

Like his father, the magistrate, he will offer neutrality before launching into dissent. "I'm ready to admit," he will begin, or "I don't want to take over the whole conversation . . ." Sometimes the sentence comes to nothing. Like his father, he lets his eyelids droop, tries to speak lightly and slowly. The magistrate is famous for fading out of a discussion by slow degrees. At one time he was said to be the youngest magistrate ever to fall asleep in court: he would black out when he thought he wasn't needed and snap to just as the case turned around. Apparently, he never missed a turning. He has described his own mind to Pascal: it is like a superlatively smooth car with an invisible driver in control. The driver is the magistrate's unconscious will.

To Pascal a mind is a door, ajar or shut. His grades are good, but this side of brilliant. He has a natural gift—a precise, perfectly etched memory. How will he use it? He thinks he could as easily become an actor as a lawyer. When he tells his parents so, they seem not to mind. He could turn into an actor-manager, with a private theatre of his own, or the director of one of the great national theatres, commissioning new work, refurbishing the classics, settling questions at issue with a word or two.

The Brouets are tolerant parents, ready for anything. They met for the first time in May of 1968, a few yards away from a barricade of burning cars. She had a stone in her hand; when she saw him looking at her, she put it down. They walked up the Boulevard Saint-Michel together, and he told her his plan for reforming the judiciary. He was a bit older, about twenty-six. Answering his question, she said she was from Alsace. He reminded her how the poet Paul Éluard had picked up his future wife in the street, on a rainy evening. She was from Alsace, too, and starving, and in a desperate, muddled, amateurish way pretending to be a prostitute.

Well, this was not quite the same story. In 1968 the future Mme. Brouet was studying to be an analyst of handwriting, with employment to follow—so she had been promised—in the personnel section of a large department store. In the meantime, she was staying with a Protestant Reformed Church pastor and his family in Rue Fustel-de-Coulanges. She had been on her way home to dinner when she stopped to pick up the stone. She had a mother in Alsace, and a little brother, Amedée—"Dédé."

"Sylvie and I have known both sides of the barricades," the magistrate likes to say, now. What he means is that they cannot be crowded into a political corner. The stone in the hand has made her a rebel, at least in his recollections. She never looks at a newspaper, because of her reputation for being against absolutely everything. So he says, but perhaps it isn't exact: she looks at the pages marked "Culture," to see what is on at the galleries. He reads three morning papers at breakfast and, if he has time, last evening's *Le Monde*. Reading, he narrows his eyes. Sometimes he looks as though everything he thinks and believes had been translated into a foreign language and, suddenly, back again.

When Pascal was about nine, his father said, "What do you suppose you will do, one day?"

They were at breakfast. Pascal's Uncle Amedée was there. Like everyone else, Pascal called him Dédé. Pascal looked across at him and said, "I want to be a bachelor, like Dédé."

His mother moaned, "Oh, no!" and covered her face. The magistrate waited until she had recovered before speaking. She looked up, smiling, a bit embarrassed. Then he explained, slowly and carefully, that Dédé was too young to be considered a bachelor. He was a student, a youth. "A student, a student," he repeated, thinking perhaps that if he kept saying it Dédé would study hard.

Dédé had a button of a nose that looked ridiculous on someone so tall, and a mass of curly fair hair. Because of the hair, the magistrate could not take him seriously; his private name for Dédé was "Harpo."

That period of Pascal's life, nine rounding to ten, was also the autumn before an important election year. The elections were five months off, but already people argued over dinner and Sunday lunch. One Sunday in October, the table was attacked by wasps, drawn in from the garden by a dish of sliced melon—the last of the season, particularly fragrant and sweet. The French doors to the garden stood open. Sunlight entered and struck through the wine decanters and dissolved in the waxed tabletop in pale red and gold. From his place, Pascal could see the enclosed garden, the apartment blocks behind it, a golden poplar tree, and the wicker chairs where the guests, earlier, had sat with their drinks.

There were two couples: the Turbins, older than Pascal's parents, and the Chevallier-Crochets, who had not been married long. Mme. Chevallier-Crochet attended an art-history course with Pascal's mother, on Thursday afternoons. They had never been here before, and were astonished to discover a secret garden in Paris with chairs, grass, a garden rake, a tree. Just as their expression of amazement was starting to run thin and patches of silence appeared, Abelarda, newly come from Cádiz, appeared at the door and called them to lunch. She said, "It's ready," though that was not what Mme. Brouet had asked her to say; at least, not that way. The guests got up, without haste. They were probably as hungry as Pascal but didn't want it to show. Abelarda went on standing, staring at the topmost leaves of the poplar, trying to remember what she ought to have said.

A few minutes later, just as they were starting to eat their melon, wasps came thudding against the table, like pebbles thrown. The adults froze, as though someone had drawn a gun. Pascal knew that sitting still was a good way to be stung. If you waved your napkin, shouted orders, the wasps might fly away. But he was not expected to give instructions; he was here, with adults, to discover how conversation is put together, how to sound interesting without being forward, amusing without seeming familiar. At that moment, Dédé did an unprecedented and courageous thing: he picked up the platter of melon, crawling with wasps, and took it outside, as far as the foot of the tree. And came back to applause: at least, his sister clapped, and young Mme. Chevallier-Crochet cried, "Bravo! Bravo!"

Dédé smiled, but, then, he was always smiling. His sister wished he wouldn't; the smile gave his brother-in-law another reason for calling him Harpo. Sitting down, he seemed to become entwined with his chair. He was too tall ever to be comfortable. He needed larger chairs, tables that were both higher and wider, so that he would not bump his knees, or put his feet on the shoes of the lady sitting opposite.

Pascal's father just said, "So, no more melon." It was something he particularly liked, and there might be none now until next summer. If Dédé had asked his opinion instead of jumping up so impulsively, he might have said, "Just leave it," and taken a chance on getting stung.

Well; no more for anyone. The guests sat a little straighter, waiting for the next course: beef, veal, or mutton, or the possibility of duck. Pascal's mother asked him to shut the French doors. She did not expect another wasp invasion, but there might be strays. Mme. Chevallier-Crochet remarked that Pascal was tall for his age, then asked what his age was. "He is almost ten," said Mme. Brouet, looking at her son with some wonder. "I can hardly believe it. I don't understand time."

Mme. Turbin said she did not have to consult a watch to know the exact time. It must be a quarter to two now. If it was, her daughter Brigitte had just landed in Salonika. Whenever her daughter boarded a plane, Mme. Turbin accompanied her in her mind, minute by minute.

"Thessalonika," M. Turbin explained.

The Chevallier-Crochets had spent their honeymoon in Sicily. If they had it to do over again, they said, they would change their minds and go to Greece.

Mme. Brouet said they would find it very different from Sicily. Her mind was on something else entirely: Abelarda. Probably Abelarda had expected them to linger over a second helping of melon. Perhaps she was sitting in the kitchen with nothing to do, listening to a program of Spanish music on the radio. Mme. Brouet caught a wide-awake glance from her husband, interpreted it correctly, and went out to the kitchen to see.

One of the men turned to M. Brouet, wondering if he could throw some light on the election candidates: unfortunate stories were making the rounds. Pascal's father was often asked for information. He had connections in Paris, like stout ropes attached to the upper civil service and to politics. One sister was married to a Cabinet minister's chief of staff. Her children were taken to school in a car with a red-white-and-blue emblem. The driver could park wherever he liked. The magistrate's grandfather had begun as a lieutenant in the cavalry and died of a heart attack the day he was appointed head of a committee to oversee war graves. His portrait, as a child on a pony, hung in the dining room. The artist was said to have copied a photograph; that was why the pony looked so stiff and the colors were wrong. The room Pascal slept in had been that child's summer bedroom; the house had once been a suburban, almost a country dwelling. Now the road outside was like a highway; even with the doors shut they could hear Sunday traffic pouring across an intersection, on the way to Boulogne and the Saint-Cloud bridge.

The magistrate replied that he did not want to take over the whole conversation but he did feel safe in saying this: Several men, none of whom he had any use for, were now standing face to face. Sometimes he felt like washing his hands of the future. (Saying this, he slid his hands together.) However, before his guests could show shock or disappointment, he added, "But one cannot remain indifferent. This is an old country, an ancient civilization." Here his voice faded out. "We owe . . . One has to . . . A certain unbreakable loyalty . . ." And he placed his hands on the table, calmly, one on each side of his plate.

At that moment Mme. Brouet returned, her cheeks and forehead pink, as if she had got too close to a hot oven. Abelarda came along next, to change the plates. She was pink in the face, too.

Pascal saw the candidates lined up like rugby teams. He was allowed to watch rugby on television. His parents did not care for soccer: the players showed off, received absurd amounts of money just for kicking a ball, and there was something the matter with their shorts. "With all that money, they could buy clothes that fit," Pascal's mother had said. Rugby players were different. They were the embodiment of action and its outcome, in an ideal form. They got muddied for love of sport. France had won the Five Nations tournament, beating even the dreaded Welsh, whose fans always set up such eerie wailing in the stands. Actually, they were trying to sing. It must have been the way the early Celts joined in song before the Roman conquest, the magistrate had told Pascal.

No one at table could have made a rugby team. They were too thin. Dédé was a broomstick. Of course, Pascal played soccer at school, in a small cement courtyard. The smaller boys, aged six, seven, tried to imitate Michel Platini, but they got everything wrong. They would throw the ball high in the air and kick at nothing, leg crossed over the chest, arms spread.

The magistrate kept an eye on the dish Abelarda was now handing around: partridges in a nest of shredded cabbage—an entire surprise. Pascal looked over at Dédé, who sat smiling to himself, for no good reason. (If Pascal had continued to follow his father's gaze he might be told gently, later, that one does not stare at food.)

There was no more conversation to be had from M. Brouet, for the moment. Helping themselves to partridge, the guests told one another stories everybody knew. All the candidates were in a declining state of health and morality. One had to be given injections of ground-up Japanese seaweed; otherwise he lost consciousness, sometimes in the midst of a sentence. Others kept going on a mixture of cocaine and Vitamin C. Their private means had been acquired by investing in gay bars and foreign wars, and evicting the poor. Only the Ministry of the Interior knew the nature and extent of their undercover financial dealings. And yet some of these men had to be found better than others, if democracy was not to come to a standstill. As M. Brouet had pointed out, one cannot wash one's hands of the future.

The magistrate had begun to breathe evenly and deeply. Perhaps the sunlight beating on the panes of the shut doors made him feel drowsy.

"Étienne is never quite awake or asleep," said his wife, meaning it as a compliment.

She was proud of everyone related to her, even by marriage, and took pride in her father, who had run away from home and family to live in New Caledonia. He had shown spirit and a sense of initiative, like Dédé with the wasps. (Now that Pascal is fourteen, he has heard this often.) But pride is not the same as helpless love. The person she loved best, in that particular way, was Dédé.

Dédé had come to stay with the Brouets because his mother, Pascal's grandmother, no longer knew what to do with him. He was never loud or abrupt, never forced an opinion on anyone, but he could not be left without guidance—even though he could vote, and was old enough to do some of the things he did, such as sign his mother's name to a check. (Admittedly, only once.) This was his second visit; the first, last spring, had not sharpened his character, in spite of his brother-in-law's conversation, his sister's tender anxiety, the sense of purpose to be gained by walking his little nephew to school. Sent home to Colmar (firm handshake with the magistrate at the Gare de l'Est, tears and chocolates from his sister, presentation of an original drawing from Pascal), he had accidentally set fire to his mother's kitchen, then to his own bedclothes. Accidents, the insurance people had finally agreed, but they were not too pleased. His mother was at the present time under treatment for exhaustion, with a private nurse to whom she made expensive presents. She had about as much money sense as Harpo, the magistrate said. (Without lifting his head from his homework, Pascal could take in nearly everything uttered in the hall, on the stairs, and in two adjacent rooms.)

When they were all four at breakfast Mme. Brouet repeated her brother's name in every second sentence: wondering if Dédé wanted more toast, if someone would please pass him the strawberry jam, if he had enough blankets on his bed, if he needed an extra key. (He was a great loser of keys.) The magistrate examined his three morning papers. He did not want to have to pass anything to Harpo. Mme. Brouet was really just speaking to herself.

That autumn, Dédé worked at a correspondence course, in preparation for a competitive civil-service examination. If he was among the first dozen, eliminating perhaps hundreds of clever young men and women, he would be eligible for a post in the nation's railway system. His work would be indoors, of course; no one expected him to be out in all weathers, trudging alongside the tracks, looking for something to repair. Great artists, leaders of honor and reputation, had got their start at a desk in a railway office. Pascal's mother, whenever she said this, had to pause, as she searched her mind for their names. The railway had always been a seedbed of outstanding careers, she would continue. She would then point out to Dédé that their father had been a supervisor of public works.

After breakfast Dédé wound a long scarf around his neck and walked Pascal to school. He had invented an apartment with movable walls. Everything one needed could be got within reach by pulling a few levers or pressing a button. You could spend your life in the middle of a room without having to stir. He and Pascal refined the invention; that was what they talked about, on the way to Pascal's school. Then Dédé came home and studied until lunchtime. In the afternoon he drew new designs of his idea. Perhaps he was lonely. The doctor looking after his mother had asked him not to call or write, for the moment.


Pascal's mother believed Dédé needed a woman friend, even though he was not ready to get married. Pascal heard her say, "Art and science, architecture, culture." These were the factors that could change Dédé's life, and to which he would find access through the right kind of woman. Mme. Brouet had someone in mind—Mlle. Turbin, who held a position of some responsibility in a travel agency. She was often sent abroad to rescue visitors or check their complaints. Today's lunch had been planned around her, but at the last minute she had been called to Greece, where a tourist, bitten by a dog, had received an emergency specific for rabies, and believed the Greeks were trying to kill him.

Her parents had come, nevertheless. It was a privilege to meet the magistrate and to visit a rare old house, one of the last of its kind still in private hands. Before lunch Mme. Turbin had asked to be shown around. Mme. Brouet conducted a tour for the women, taking care not to open the door to Dédé's room: there had been a fire in a wastepaper basket only a few hours before, and everything in there was charred or singed or soaked.

At lunch, breaking out of politics, M. Turbin described the treatment the tourist in Salonika had most probably received: it was the same the world over, and incurred the use of a long needle. He held out his knife, to show the approximate length.

"Stop!" cried Mme. Chevallier-Crochet. She put her napkin over her nose and mouth; all they could see was her wild eyes. Everyone stopped eating, forks suspended—all but the magistrate, who was pushing aside shreds of cabbage to get at the last of the partridge.

M. Chevallier-Crochet explained that his wife was afraid of needles. He could not account for it; he had not known her as a child. It seemed to be a singular fear, one that set her apart. Meantime, his wife closed her eyes; opened them, though not as wide as before; placed her napkin neatly across her lap; and swallowed a piece of bread.

M. Turbin said he was sorry. He had taken it for granted that any compatriot of the great Louis Pasteur must have seen a needle or two. Needles were only a means to an end.

Mme. Brouet glanced at her husband, pleading for help, but he had just put a bite of food into his mouth. He was always last to be served when there were guests, and everything got to him cold. That was probably why he ate in such a hurry. He shrugged, meaning, Change the subject.

"Pascal," she said, turning to him. At last, she thought of something to say: "Do you remember Mlle. Turbin? Charlotte Turbin?"

"Brigitte?" said Pascal.

"I'm sure you remember," she said, not listening at all. "In the travel agency, on Rue Caumartin?"

"She gave me the corrida poster," said Pascal, wondering how this had slipped her mind.

"We went to see her, you and I, the time we wanted to go to Egypt? Now do you remember?"

"We never went to Egypt."

"No. Papa couldn't get away just then, so we finally went back to Deauville, where Papa has so many cousins. So you do remember Mlle. Turbin, with the pretty auburn hair?"

"Chestnut," said the two Turbins, together.

"My sister," said Dédé, all of a sudden, indicating her with his left hand, the right clutching a wineglass. "Before she got married, my mother told me . . ." The story, whatever it was, engulfed him in laughter. "A dog tried to bite her," he managed to say.

"You can tell us about it another time," said his sister.

He continued to laugh, softly, just to himself, while Abelarda changed the plates again.

The magistrate examined his clean new plate. No immediate surprises: salad, another plate, cheese, a dessert plate. His wife had given up on Mlle. Turbin. Really, it was his turn now, her silence said.

"I may have mentioned this before," said the magistrate. "And I would not wish to keep saying the same things over and over. But I wonder if you agree that the pivot of French politics today is no longer in France."

"The Middle East," said M. Turbin, nodding his head.

"Washington," said M. Chevallier-Crochet. "Washington calls Paris every morning and says, Do this, Do that."

"The Middle East and the Soviet Union," said M. Turbin.

"There," said M. Brouet. "We are all in agreement."

Many of the magistrate's relatives and friends thought he should be closer to government, to power. But his wife wanted him to stay where he was and get his pension. After he retired, when Pascal was grown, they would visit Tibet and the north of China, and winter in Kashmir.

"You know, this morning—" said Dédé, getting on with something that was on his mind.

"Another time," said his sister. "Never mind about this morning. It is all forgotten. Étienne is speaking, now."

This morning! The guests had no idea, couldn't begin to imagine what had taken place, here, in the dining room, at this very table. Dédé had announced, overjoyed, "I've got my degree." For Dédé was taking a correspondence course that could not lead to a degree of any kind. It must have been just his way of trying to stop studying so that he could go home.

"Degree?" The magistrate folded yesterday's *Le Monde* carefully before putting it down. "What do you mean, degree?"

Pascal's mother got up to make fresh coffee. "I'm glad to hear it, Dédé," she said.

"A degree in what?" said the magistrate.

Dédé shrugged, as if no one had bothered to tell him. "It came just the other day," he said. "I've got my degree, and now I can go home."

"Is there something you could show us?"

"There was just a letter, and I lost it," said Dédé. "A real diploma costs two thousand francs. I don't know where I'd find the money."

The magistrate did not seem to disbelieve; that was because of his training. But then he said, "You began your course about a month ago?"

# Dédé

"I had been thinking about it for a long time," said Dédé.

"And now they have awarded you a degree. You are perfectly right—it's time you went home. You can take the train tonight. I'll call your mother."

Pascal's mother returned, carrying a large white coffeepot. "I wonder where your first job will be," she said.

Why were she and her brother so remote from things as they are? Perhaps because of their mother, the grandmother in Colmar. Once, she had taken Pascal by the chin and tried to force him to look her in the eye. She had done it to her children. Pascal knows, now, that you cannot have your chin held in a vise and undividedly meet a blue stare. Somewhere at the back of the mind is a second self with eyes tight shut. Dédé and his sister could seem to meet any glance, even the magistrate's when he was being most nearly wide awake. They seemed to be listening, but the person he thought he was talking to, trying to reach the heart of, was deaf and blind. Pascal's mother listens when she needs to know what might happen next.

All Pascal understood, for the moment, was that when Dédé had mentioned taking a degree, he was saying something he merely wished were true.

"We'll probably never see you, once you start to work," said Pascal's mother, pouring Dédé's coffee.

The magistrate looked as if such great good luck was not to be expected. Abelarda, who had gone upstairs to make the beds, screamed from the head of the staircase that Dédé's room was full of smoke.


Abelarda moved slowly around the table carrying a plum tart, purple and gold, caramelized all over its surface, and a bowl of cream. Mme. Turbin glanced at the tart and shook her head no: M. Turbin was not allowed sugar now, and she had got out of the habit of eating desserts. It seemed unfair to tempt him.

It was true, her husband said. She had even given up making sweets, on his account. He described her past achievements—her famous chocolate mousse with candied bitter orange peel, her celebrated pineapple flan.

"My semolina crown mold with apricot sauce," she said. "I must have given the recipe away a hundred times."

Mme. Chevallier-Crochet wondered if she could have a slice half the size of the wedge Abelarda had already prepared. Abelarda put down the bowl of cream and divided the wedge in half. The half piece was still too much; Abelarda said it could not be cut again without breaking into a mess of crumbs. M. Chevallier-Crochet said to his wife, "For God's sake, just take it and leave what you can't eat." Mme. Chevallier-Crochet replied that everything she said and did seemed to be wrong, she had better just sit here and say and do nothing. Abelarda, crooning encouragement, pushed onto her plate a fragment of pastry and one plum.

"No cream," she said, too late.

Mme. Brouet looked at the portrait of her husband's grandfather, then at her son, perhaps seeking a likeness. Sophie Chevallier-Crochet had seemed lively and intelligent at their history-of-art class. Mme. Brouet had never met the husband before, and was unlikely ever to lay eyes on him again. She accepted large portions of tart and cream, to set an example, in case the other two ladies had inhibited the men.

M. Turbin, after having made certain that no extra sugar had been stirred into the cream, took more cream than tart. His wife, watching him closely, sipped water over her empty plate. "It's only fruit," he said.

The magistrate helped himself to all the crumbs and fragments of burnt sugar on the dish. He rattled the spoon in the bowl of cream, scraping the sides; there was nearly none left. It was the fault of M. Chevallier-Crochet, who had gone on filling his plate, as though in a dream, until Abelarda moved the bowl away.

The guests finished drinking their coffee at half past four, and left at a quarter to five. When they had gone, Mme. Brouet lay down—not on a couch or a settee but on the living-room floor. She stared at the ceiling and told Pascal to leave her alone.

# Dédé

Abelarda, Dédé, and the magistrate were up in Dédé's room. Abelarda helped him pack. Late that night, the magistrate drove him to the Gare de l'Est.


Dédé came back to Paris about a year ago. He is said to be different now. He has a part-time job with a television polling service: every day he is given a list of telephone numbers in the Paris area and he calls them to see what people were watching the night before and which program they wish they had watched instead. His mother has bought him a one-room place overlooking Parc de Montsouris. The Brouets have never tried to get in touch with him or invited him to a meal. Dédé's Paris—unknown, foreign almost—lies at an unmapped distance from Pascal's house.

One night, not long ago, when they all three were having dinner, Pascal said, "What if Dédé just came to the door?" He meant the front door, of course, but his parents glanced at the glass doors and the lamps reflected in the dark panes, so that night was screened from sight. Pascal imagined Dédé standing outside, watching and smiling, with that great mop of hair.

He is almost as tall as Dédé, now. Perhaps his father had not really taken notice of his height—it came about so gradually— but when Pascal got up to draw a curtain across the doors that night at dinner, his father looked at him as if he were suddenly setting a value on the kind of man he might become. It was a steady look, neither hot nor cold. For a moment Pascal said to himself, He will never fall asleep again. As for his mother, she sat smiling and dreaming, still hoping for some reason to start loving Dédé once more.

# KINGDOM COME

After having spent twenty-four years in the Republic of Saltnatek, where he established the first modern university, recorded the vocabulary and structure of the Saltnatek tongue, and discovered in a remote village an allophylian language unknown except to its speakers, Dr. Dominic Missierna returned to Europe to find that nobody cared. Saltnatek was neither lush nor rich nor seductive, nor poor enough to arouse international pity. The university survived on grants left over from the defense budget, and even Missierna had to admit he had not attracted teachers of the first order. He had wasted his vitality chasing money for salaries and equipment, up to the day when an ungrateful administration dismissed him and the latest revolutionary council, thanking him for nothing, put him on a plane.

He was still in mourning for his Saltnatek years. It grieved him to hear, at a linguistic congress in Helsinki, younger colleagues in the most offhand way confusing Saltnatek with Malta and Madagascar. Saltnatek consisted of an archipelago of naked islands, one of which had been a port of call for cruise ships early in the century. Most tourists had not even bothered to go ashore: there was nothing to admire except straight rows of undecorated houses, and nothing to buy except shells of giant sea snails, on which the nation's artists had carved in a spiral pattern WHEN THIS YOU SEE, REMEMBER ME. The motto was thought to have been copied from the lid of a snuffbox found in the pocket of a drowned naval officer during the Napoleonic wars. (Missierna supposed the box was probably a lucky piece, even though it had not turned out to be providential. He kept this to himself; he was not in the business of offering speculations.) Even that trifling commerce had come to a stop when, just after the First World War, a society for the protection of sea snails urged a boycott of mutilated shells—a prohibition that caused Saltnatek great bewilderment and economic distress.

In Helsinki, his heart galloping, his voice trembling sometimes, Missierna disclosed the existence of a complex and living language, spoken by an inbred population that produced children of much thievishness, cunning, and blank beauty. He stood on a stage too large for him, fuzzily lighted, in an auditorium the size of a concert hall. Nine men and three women sat, singly, in the first fifteen rows. They were still and unresponsive, and as soon as he had finished reading they got up in the same quiet way and filed out. There were no questions: he had brought back to Europe one more system, and no one knew how to make the old ones work.

If he was disappointed, it was in part because he was no longer young, and it was almost too late for his competence, perhaps his genius, to receive the rewards it deserved. Although he was far less vain than any of the substandard teachers he had interviewed and hired for Saltnatek, he still hoped that at least one conclusion might be named for him, so that his grandchildren, coming across his name in a textbook, could say, "So this is what he was like—modest, creative." But all that anyone said at the Helsinki congress was "You have demonstrated nothing that cannot be shown through Hungarian."

During the years when he was so obsessively occupied, Europe had grown small, become depleted, as bald in spirit as Saltnatek's sandy and stony islands. The doubting voices were thin and metallic. No one was listening. His colleagues said, "One step after the other," and "One at a time." They trod upon discarded rules of address, raked the ground to find shreds of sense and reason. Salvation was in the dust or it was nowhere. Even if he were to reveal twenty new and orderly and poetic methods of creating order by means of words, he would be told, "We had better deal with matters underfoot, closer to home."

He was a divorced parent, which meant he had children and grandchildren but no place in particular to go. Saltnatek had been like a child, and he had stayed with it longer than with any other, had seen it into maturity, and it had used and rejected him, as children do, as it is their right. It was not in his nature to put out emotional ultimatums. In the past, it could have been his business—he should have made it his business—to observe the patterns of exchange among his real children, even if the information, tabulated, had left him depressed and frightened. He could have taken them as an independent republic and applied for entry. Even now, he considered inviting himself for next Christmas. He would surely obtain the limited visa no one dares refuse a homeless old man, a distinguished relative, not poor, needing only consideration—notice taken of his deafness, his stiff shoulder, his need to get up and eat breakfast at five o'clock, his allergies to butter and white wine.

What to take on the Christmas exploration? The first rule of excursions into uncankered societies is: Don't bring presents. Not unless one wants to face charges of corruption. But then, like any scholar fending off a critic, he could justify the gifts, telling himself that another visitor might taint the society in a manner deadlier still, whereas he, Missierna, sat lightly. He had been a featherweight on his children; he had scarcely gone near them. A present from parent to child surely reinforces a natural tie. When they were young, he used to bring home one wristwatch and make them draw lots. For professional trips he had packed radio batteries; his travels had taught him that new republics run out of them soon. He had taken ski boots wherever there were snowy mountains, except in places where snow was sacred. He had always shown a sense of patience, a good-tempered approach to time, as he cut through the thorn patch of transit visas, six-month-residence permits, five-year research grants. To enter one's own family, he supposed, one needed to fill out forms. All he would have to understand was the slant of the questions.

From his hotel room in Helsinki, Missierna saw the Baltic and gulls skimming over the whitecaps. At night ghosts floated along the horizon. He took it for granted they were ghosts—having lived among people who saw a great many—and not simply the white shadows of summer.

An insurance actuarial study gave him six more years to live if he went on as he was, eight if he gave up smoking, nine and a half if he adopted an optimistic outlook. What about white magic? What about trying to add a few more summer nights by means of poems and incantations? Why not appeal to a saint—a saint so obscure that the direct line from Missierna's mind to the saint's memory of a mind would be clean, without the clutter of other, alien voices? He could begin by repeating his own name, before deciding what conjury should come next.

His grandchildren surely lived on magic. There was fresh daylight every morning. Clothes dropped on the floor were found clean and folded. A gray-haired man at the congress, who said he had once been Missierna's student, had told him that very soon, by law, children were going to be asked to acknowledge their parents, instead of the other way. There would be some cold refusals, Missierna supposed, and some selfish ones, and some inspired by embarrassment. There might be cases of simple antipathy, too. Most children would probably accept their parents, out of pity, or to keep a strong thread of filiation, or to claim an inheritance, or to conform to an astral pattern. Some, to avoid the sight of adult tears. A few might show the blind trust that parents pray for. The new insecurity, the terror of being cast off, was already causing adults to adopt the extreme conservatism that is usually characteristic of the very young. A mistrust of novelty and change surely accounted for Missierna's sparse audience, the silence in the auditorium, the unwillingness to know something more.

In Saltnatek, toward the end, he had heard some of the cool remarks that said, plainly, he was not a father; heard them from students he had taught, reared, nurtured, and who now were ready to send him packing: "You can't say we didn't warn you." "I tried to tell you that someday you'd be sorry." "I'm sorry if you're sorry. But that's all I have to be sorry about." From his own children there had been monitory signals, too, which he had mistaken for pertness: "Can't you ask a waitress for a cup of coffee without telling your life story?" "Other parents don't take the wrong bus." "Please don't get up and dance. It makes you look so silly." Their eyes were clean, pure, but bedevilled by unease and mortification. The eyes of children are the eyes of petit bourgeois, he decided. They can't help it; they are born wondering if their parents are worth what the bus driver thinks.

For twenty-four years the eyes of Saltnatek had appraised him, and had then turned away. He had become to himself large and awkward—a parent without authority, dispossessed, left to stumble around in an airport, as if he were sick or drunk.

He could still recite by rote the first test sentences he had used for his research:

"Now that you mention it, I see what you mean."

"There is no law against it, is there?"

"I am not comfortable, but I hope to be comfortable soon."

"Anyone may write to him. He answers all letters."

"Look it up. You will see that I was right all along."

At the outset, in Saltnatek, he had asked for a governmental ruling to put a clamp on the language: the vocabulary must not grow during the period of his field work. Expansion would confuse the word count. They had not been sure what to call him. Some had said "Father," which was close in sound to his name, as they pronounced it. His own children had for a while avoided saying even "you," dropping from their greetings such sentences as "What did you bring us?" and "Are you staying long?" They were like long-term patients in a hospital, or rebels interned. Their expression, at once careful and distant, seemed to be telling him, "If you intend to keep coming and going, then at least bring us something we need."

His children were not proud of him. It was his own fault; he had not told them enough. Perhaps he seemed old, but he appeared young to himself. In the shaving mirror he saw the young man he had been at university. In his dreams, even his bad dreams, he was never more than twenty-one.

Saltnatek was his last adventure. He would turn to his true children, whether they welcomed the old explorer or not. Or he could find something else to do—something tranquil; he could watch Europe as it declined and sank, with its pettiness and faded cruelty, its crabbed richness and sentimentality. Something might be discovered out of shabbiness—some measure taken of the past and the present, now that they were ground and trampled to the same shape and size. But what if he had lost his mixture of duty and curiosity, his professional humility, his ruthlessness? In that case, he could start but he would never finish.

At Helsinki he heard young colleagues describing republics they had barely seen. They seemed to have been drawn here and there for casual, private reasons. He did not like the reasons, and he regretted having mentioned, in his lecture, sibling incest in that village in Saltnatek. He had been careful to admit he had relied on folklore and legends, and would never know what went on when the children tore all their clothes off. Repeated actions are religious, but with children one can never decide if they are heathen, atheistic, agnostic, pantheistic, animist; if there remains a vestige of a ritual, a rattled-off prayer.

Say that he used his grandchildren as a little-known country: he would need to scour their language for information. What did they say when they thought "infinity"? In Saltnatek, in the village, they had offered him simple images—a light flickering, a fire that could not be doused, a sun that rose and set in long cycles, a bright night. Everything and nothing.

Perhaps they were right, and only the present moment exists, he thought. How they view endlessness is their own business. But if I start minding my own business, he said to himself, I have no more reason to be.

Was there any cause to feel uneasy about the present moment in Europe? What was wrong with it? There was no quarrel between Wales and Turkey. Italy and Schleswig-Holstein were not at war. It was years since some part of the population, running away, had dug up and carried off its dead. It seemed to him now that his life's labor—the digging out, the coaxing and bribing to arrive at secret meanings—amounted to exhumation and flight.

The village children had wanted white crash helmets and motorcycles. He had given them helmets but said he could not bring in the bikes, which were dangerous, which would make the ancient windows rattle and the babies cry. Besides, there were no roads. Some of the village women turned the helmets into flowerpots, but the helmets were airtight, there was no drainage, the plants died. The helmets would never rot. Only the maimed giant snails, thrown back into the ocean, could decay. Missierna, the day he resolved that helmets do not die, and so have no hope of resurrection, wondered whether the time had come to stop thinking.

He should not have mentioned in his lecture that the village children were of blank but unusual beauty, that they wanted steep new roads and motorcycles. It might induce plodding, leaden, salacious scholars to travel there and seduce them, and to start one more dull and clumsy race.

All this he thought late at night in his hotel room and in the daytime as he walked the streets of Helsinki. He visited the Saltnatek consulate, because he was curiously forlorn, like a parent prevented by court order from having any more say in his children's fate and education. He entered a bookstore said to be the largest in Europe, and a department store that seemed to be its most expensive. On a street corner he bought chocolate ice cream in a plastic cone. He did not return the cone, as he was supposed to. He believed he had paid for it. He crossed a busy road, saying to himself, "The cone is mine. I'm not giving it up."

So—he had become grasping. This slight, new, interesting evaluation occupied his mind for some minutes. Why keep the cone? It would be thrown away even in Saltnatek, even in the poorest, meanest dwelling. Children in their collective vision now wanted buses without drivers, planes without pilots, lessons without teachers. Wanted to come into the world knowing how to write and count, or never to know—it was all the same conundrum. Or to know only a little about everything. He saw helmets on a window ledge, ferns growing out of them. By now, the women had been taught to use pebbles for drainage. Saw children tearing uphill on the motorcycles other visitors had brought. Imagining this, or believing he could see it—the two were identical—he understood that he would never go back, even if they would have him. He would live out his six actuarial years on his own half-continent. He would imagine, or think he could see, its pillars rotting, seaweed swirling round the foundations. He would breathe the used-up air that stank of dead sea life. He might have existed a few days past his six more years in the clearer air of Saltnatek. Then? Have fallen dead at the feet of the vacant, thievish children, heard for a second longer than life allows the cadence of their laughter when they mocked him—the decaying, inquisitive old stranger, still trying to trick them into giving away their word for Kingdom Come.

# ACROSS THE BRIDGE

We were walking over the bridge from the Place de la Concorde, my mother and I—arm in arm, like two sisters who never quarrel. She had the invitations to my wedding in a leather shopping bag: I was supposed to be getting married to Arnaud Pons. My father's first cousin, Gaston Castelli, deputy for a district in the South, had agreed to frank the envelopes. He was expecting us at the Palais Bourbon, at the other end of the bridge. His small office looked out on nothing of interest—just a wall and some windows. A typist who did not seem to work for anyone in particular sat outside his door. He believed she was there to spy on him, and for that reason had told my mother to keep the invitations out of sight.

I had been taken to see him there once or twice. On the wall were two photographs of Vincent Auriol, President of the Republic, one of them signed, and a picture of the restaurant where Jean Jaurès was shot to death; it showed the façade and the waiters standing in the street in their long white aprons. For furniture he had a Louis Philippe armchair, with sticking plaster around all four legs, a lumpy couch covered with a blanket, and, for visitors, a pair of shaky varnished chairs filched from another room. When the Assembly was in session he slept on the couch. (Deputies were not supposed actually to live on the premises, but some of those from out of town liked to save on hotel bills.) His son Julien was fighting in Indochina. My mother had already cautioned me to ask how Julien was getting along and when he thought the war would be over. Only a few months earlier she might have hinted about a wedding when Julien came back, pretending to make a joke of it, but it was too late now for insinuations: I was nearly at the altar with someone else. My marrying Julien was a thought my parents and Cousin Gaston had enjoyed. In some way, we would have remained their children forever.

When Cousin Gaston came to dinner he and Papa discussed their relations in Nice and the decadent state of France. Women were not expected to join in: Maman always found a reason to go off to the kitchen and talk things over with Claudine, a farm girl from Normandy she had trained to cook and wait. Claudine was about my age, but Maman seemed much freer with her than with me; she took it for granted that Claudine was informed about all the roads and corners of life. Having no excuse to leave, I would examine the silver, the pattern on my dinner plate, my own hands. The men, meanwhile, went on about the lowering of morality and the lack of guts of the middle class. They split over what was to be done: our cousin was a Socialist, though not a fierce one. He saw hope in the new postwar managerial generation, who read Marx without becoming dogmatic Marxists, while my father thought the smart postwar men would be swept downhill along with the rest of us.

Once, Cousin Gaston mentioned why his office was so seedily fitted out. It seemed that the government had to spend great sums on rebuilding roads; they had gone to pieces during the war and, of course, were worse today. Squads of German prisoners of war sent to put them right had stuffed the road beds with leaves and dead branches. As the underlay began to rot, the surfaces had collapsed. Now repairs were made by French work-ers—unionized, Communist-led, always on the verge of a na-tional strike. There was no money left over.

"There never has been any money left over," Papa said. "When there is, they keep it quiet."

He felt uneasy about the franking business. The typist in the hall might find out and tell a reporter on one of the opposition weeklies. The reporter would then write a blistering piece on nepotism and the misuse of public funds, naming names. (My mother never worried. She took small favors to be part of the grace of life.)

It was hot on the bridge, July in April. We still wore our heavy coats. Too much good weather was not to be trusted. There were no clouds over the river, but just the kind of firm blue sky I found easy to paint. Halfway across, we stopped to look at a boat with strings of flags, and tourists sitting along the bank. Some of the men had their shirts off. I stared at the water and saw how far below it was and how cold it looked, and I said, "If I weren't a Catholic, I'd throw myself in."

"Sylvie!"—as if she had lost me in a crowd.

"We're going to so much trouble," I said. "Just so I can marry a man I don't love."

"How do you know you don't love him?"

"I'd know if I did."

"You haven't tried," she said. "It takes patience, like practic-ing scales. Don't you want a husband?"

"Not Arnaud."

"What's wrong with Arnaud?"

"I don't know."

"Well," after a pause, "what *do* you know?"

"I want to marry Bernard Brunelle. He lives in Lille. His father owns a big textile business—the factories, everything. We've been writing. He doesn't know I'm engaged."

"Brunelle? Brunelle? Textiles? From Lille? It sounds like a mistake. In Lille they just marry each other, and textiles marry textiles."

"I've got one thing right," I said. "I want to marry Bernard."

My mother was a born coaxer and wheedler; avoided confrontation, preferring to move to a different terrain and beckon, smiling. One promised nearly anything just to keep the smile on her face. She was slim and quick, like a girl of fourteen. My father liked her in flowered hats, so she still wore the floral bandeaux with their wisps of veil that had been fashionable ten years before. Papa used to tell about a funeral service where Maman had removed her hat so as to drape a mantilla over her hair. An usher, noticing the hat beside her on the pew, had placed it with the other flowers around the coffin. When I repeated the story to Arnaud he said the floral-hat anecdote was one of the world's oldest. He had heard it a dozen times, always about a different funeral. I could not see why Papa would go on telling it if it were not true, or why Maman would let him. Perhaps she was the first woman it had ever happened to.

"You say that Bernard has written to you," she said, in her lightest, prettiest, most teasing manner. "But where did he send the letters? Not to the house. I'd have noticed."

No conspirator gives up a network that easily. Mine consisted of Chantal Nauzan, my trusted friend, the daughter of a general my father greatly admired. Recently Papa had begun saying that if I had been a boy he might have wanted a career in the Army for me. As I was a girl, he did not want me to do anything too particular or specific. He did not want to have to say, "My daughter is . . ." or "Sylvie does . . ." because it might make me sound needy or plain.

"Dear Sylvie," my mother went on. "Look at me. Let me see your eyes. Has he written 'marriage' in a letter signed with his name?" I looked away. What a question! "Would you show me the letter—the important one? I promise not to read the whole thing." I shook my head no. I was not sharing Bernard. She moved to new ground, so fast I could barely keep up. "And you would throw yourself off a bridge for him?"

"Just in my thoughts," I said. "I think about it when Arnaud makes me listen to records—all those stories about women dying, Brünnhilde and Mimi and Butterfly. I think that for the rest of my life I'll be listening to records and remembering Bernard. It's all I have to look forward to, because it is what you and Papa want."

"No," she said. "It is not at all what we want." She placed the leather bag on the parapet and turned it upside down over the river, using both hands. I watched the envelopes fall in a slow shower and land on the dark water and float apart. Strangers leaned on the parapet and stared, too, but nobody spoke.

"Papa will know what to do next," she said, altogether calmly, giving the bag a final shake. "For the time being, don't write any more letters and don't mention Bernard. Not to anyone."

I could not have defined her tone or expression. She behaved as if we had put something over on life, or on men; but that may be what I have read into it since. I looked for a clue, wondering how she wanted me to react, but she had started to walk on, making up the story we would tell our cousin, still waiting in his office to do us a good turn. (In the end, she said the wedding had to be postponed owing to a death in Arnaud's family.)

"Papa won't be able to have M. Pons as a friend now," she remarked. "He's going to miss him. I hope your Monsieur Brunelle in Lille can make up the loss."

"I have never met him," I said.

I could see white patches just under the surface of the river, quite far along. They could have been candy papers or scraps of rubbish from a barge. Maman seemed to be studying the current, too. She said, "I'm not asking you to tell me how you met him."

"In the Luxembourg Gardens. I was sketching the beehives."

"You made a nice watercolor from that sketch. I'll have it framed. You can hang it in your bedroom."

Did she mean now or after I was married? I was taller than she was: when I turned my head, trying to read her face, my eyes were level with her smooth forehead and the bandeau of daisies she was wearing that day. She said, "My girl," and took my hand—not possessively but as a sort of welcome. I was her kind, she seemed to be telling me, though she had never broken an engagement that I knew. Another of my father's stories was how she had proposed to him, had chased and cornered him and made the incredible offer. He was a young doctor then, new to Paris. Now he was an ear specialist with a large practice. His office and secretary and waiting room were in a separate wing of the apartment. When the windows were open, in warm weather, we could hear him laughing and joking with Melle Coutard, the secretary. She had been with him for years and kept his accounts; he used to say she knew all his bad secrets. My mother's people thought he was too Southern, too easily amused, too loud in his laughter. My Castelli great-grandparents had started a wholesale fruit business, across from the old bus terminal at Nice. The whole block was empty now and waiting to be torn down, so that tall buildings could replace the ochre warehouses and stores with their dark-red roofs. CASTELLI was still painted over a doorway, in faded blue. My father had worked hard to lose his local accent, which sounded comical in Paris and prevented patients from taking him seriously, but it always returned when he was with Cousin Gaston. Cousin Gaston cherished his own accent, polished and refined it: his voters mistrusted any voice that sounded north of Marseilles.

I cannot say what was taking place in the world that spring; my father did not like to see young women reading newspapers. Echoes from Indochina came to me, and news of our cousin Julien drifted around the family, but the war itself was like the murmur of a radio in a distant room. I know that it was the year of *Imperial Violets*, with Luis Mariano singing the lead. At intermission he came out to the theatre lobby, where his records were on sale, and autographed programs and record sleeves. I bought "Love Is a Bouquet of Violets," and my mother and I got in line, but when my turn came I said my name so softly that she had to repeat it for me. After the performance he took six calls and stood for a long time throwing kisses.

My mother said, "Don't start to dream about Mariano, Sylvie. He's an actor. He may not mean a word he says about love."

I was not likely to. He was too old for me, and I supposed that actors were nice to everybody in the same way. I wanted plenty of children and a husband who would always be there, not travelling and rehearsing. I wanted him to like me more than other people. I dreamed about Bernard Brunelle. I was engaged to Arnaud Pons.

Arnaud was the son of another man my father admired, I think more than anyone else. They had got to know each other through one of my father's patients, a M. Tarre. My father had treated him for a chronically abscessed ear—eight appointments—and, at the end, when M. Tarre asked if he wanted a check at once or preferred to send a bill, my father answered that he took cash, and on the nail. M. Tarre inquired if that was his usual custom. My father said it was the custom of every specialist he had ever heard of, on which M. Tarre threatened to drag him before an ethics committee. "And your secretary, too!" he shouted. We could hear him in the other wing. "Your accomplice in felony!" My mother pulled me away from the window and said I was to go on being nice to Melle Coutard.

It turned out that M. Tarre was retired from the Ministry of Health and knew all the rules. Papa calmed him down by agreeing to meet a lawyer M. Tarre knew, called Alexandre Pons. He liked the sound of the name, which had a ring of the South. Even when it turned out that those particular Ponses had been in Paris for generations, my father did not withdraw his good will.

M. Pons arrived a few days later, along with M. Tarre, who seemed to have all the time in the world. He told my father that a reprimand from an ethics committee was nothing compared with a charge of tax fraud. Imagine, M. Pons said, a team of men in English-style suits pawing over your accounts. He turned to his friend Tarre and continued, "Over yours, too. Once they get started."

M. Tarre said that his life was a house of glass, anyone was welcome to look inside, but after more remarks from M. Pons, and a couple of generous suggestions from my father, he agreed to let the thing drop.

As a way of thanking M. Pons, as well as getting to know him better, Papa asked my mother to invite him to dinner. For some reason, M. Pons waited several days before calling to say he had a wife. She turned out to be difficult, I remember, telling how she had fainted six times in eighteen months, and announcing, just as the roast lamb was served, that the smell of meat made her feel sick. However, when my mother discovered there was also a Pons son, aged twenty-six, unmarried, living at home, and working in the legal department of a large maritime-insurance firm, she asked them again, this time with Arnaud.

During the second dinner Maman said, "Sylvie is something of an artist. Everything on the dining-room walls is Sylvie's work."

Arnaud looked around, briefly. He was silent, though not shy, with a thin face and brown hair. His mind was somewhere else, perhaps in livelier company. He ate everything on his plate, sometimes frowning; when it was something he seemed to like, his expression cleared. He glanced at me, then back at my depictions of the Roman countryside and the harbor at Naples in 1850. I was sure he could see they were replicas and that he knew the originals, and perhaps despised me.

"They are only copies," I managed to say.

"But full of feeling," said Maman.

He nodded, as if acknowledging a distant and somewhat forward acquaintance—a look neither cold nor quite welcoming. I wondered what his friends were like and if they had to pass a special test before he would consent to conversation.

After dinner, in the parlor, there was the usual difficulty over coffee. Claudine was slow to serve, and particularly slow to collect the empty cups. A chinoiserie table stood just under the chandelier, but Maman made sure nothing ever was placed on it. She found an excuse to call attention to the marble floor, because she took pleasure in the icy look of it, but no one picked up the remark. Mme. Pons was first to sit down. She put her cup on the floor, crossed her legs, and tapped her foot to some tune playing in her head. Perhaps she was recalling an evening before her marriage when she had danced wearing a pleated skirt and ropes of beads: I had seen pictures of my mother dressed that way.

I had settled my own cup predicament by refusing coffee. Now I took a chair at some distance from Mme. Pons: I guessed she would soon snap out of her dream and start to ask personal questions. I looked at my hands and saw they were stained with paint. I sat on them: nobody paid attention.

My mother was showing Arnaud loose sketches and unframed watercolors of mine that she kept in a folder—more views of Italy, copies, and scenes in Paris parks drawn from life.

"Take one! Take one!" she cried.

My father went over to see what kind of taste Arnaud had. He had picked the thing nearest him, a crayon drawing of Vesuvius—not my best work. My father laughed, and said my idea of a volcano in eruption was like a haystack on fire.


Bernard's father did not respond to my father's first approach—a letter that began: "I understand that our two children, Bernard and Sylvie, are anxious to unite their destinies." Probably he was too busy finding out if we were solvent, Papa said.

My mother cancelled the wedding dates, civil and church. There were just a few presents that had to be returned to close relatives. The names of the other guests had dissolved in the Seine. "It should be done quickly," she had told my father, once the sudden change had been explained half a dozen times and he was nearly over the shock. He wondered if haste had anything to do with disgrace, though he could hardly believe it of me. No, no, nothing like that, she said. She wanted to see me safe and settled and in good hands. Well, of course, he wanted something like that, too.

As for me, I was sure I had been put on earth to marry Bernard Brunelle and move to Lille and live in a large stone house. ("Brick," my friend Chantal corrected, when I told her. "It's all brick up in Lille.") A whole floor would be given over to my children's nurseries and bedrooms and classrooms. They would learn English, Russian, German, and Italian. There would be tutors and governesses, holidays by the sea, ponies to ride, birth-day parties with huge pink cakes, servants wearing white gloves. I had never known anyone who lived exactly that way, but my vision was so precise and highly colored that it had to be prompted from Heaven. I saw the curtains in the children's rooms, and their smooth hair and clear eyes, and their neat schoolbooks. I knew it might rain in Lille, day after day: I would never complain. The weather would be part of my enchanted life.

By this time, of course, Arnaud had been invited by my father to have an important talk. But then my father balked, saying he would undertake nothing unless my mother was there. After all, I had two parents. He thought of inviting Arnaud to lunch in a restaurant—Lipp, say, so noisy and crowded that any shock Arnaud showed would not be noticed. Maman pointed out that one always ended up trying to shout over the noise, so there was a danger of being overheard. In the end, Papa asked him to come round to the apartment, at about five o'clock. He arrived with daffodils for my mother and a smaller bunch for me. He believed Papa was planning a change in the marriage contract: he would buy an apartment for us outright instead of granting a twenty-year loan, adjustable to devaluation or inflation, interest free.

They received him in the parlor, standing, and Maman handed

him the sealed rejection she had helped me compose. If I had written the narrowest kind of exact analysis it would have been: "I have tried to love you, and can't. My feelings toward you are cordial and full of respect. If you don't want me to hate the sight of you, please go away." I think that is the truth about any such failure, but nobody says it. In any case, Maman would not have permitted such a thing. She had dictated roundabout excuses, ending with a wish for his future happiness. What did we mean by happiness for Arnaud? I suppose, peace of mind.

Papa walked over to the window and stood drumming on the pane. He made some unthinking remark—that he could see part of the Church of Saint-Augustin, the air was so clear. In fact, thick, gray, lashing rain obscured everything except the nearest rank of trees.

Arnaud looked up from the letter and said, "I must be dreaming." His clever, melancholy face was the color of the rain. My mother was afraid he would faint, as Mme. Pons so liked doing, and hurt his head on the marble floor. The chill of the marble had worked through everyone's shoes. She tried to edge the men over to a carpet, but Arnaud seemed paralyzed. Filling in silence, she went on about the floor: the marble came from Italy; people had warned her against it; it was hard to keep clean and it held the cold.

Arnaud stared at his own feet, then hers. Finally, he asked where I was.

"Sylvie has withdrawn from worldly life," my mother said. I had mentioned nothing in my letter about marrying another man, so he asked a second, logical question: Was I thinking of becoming a nun?

The rain, dismantling chestnut blossoms outside, sounded like gravel thrown against the windows. I know, because I was in my bedroom, just along the passage. I could not see him then as someone frozen and stunned. He was an obstacle on a railway line. My tender and competent mother had agreed to push him off the track.

That evening I said, "What if his parents turn up here and try to make a fuss?"

"They wouldn't dare," she said. "You were more than they had ever dreamed of."

It was an odd, new way of considering the Ponses. Until then, their education and background and attention to things of the past had made up for an embarrassing lack of foresight: they had never acquired property for their only son to inherit. They lived in the same dim apartment, in a lamentable quarter, which they had first rented in 1926, the year of their marriage. It was on a street filled with uninviting stores and insurance offices, east of the Saint-Lazare station, near the old German church. (Arnaud had taken me to the church for a concert of recorded music. I had never been inside a Protestant church before. It was spare and bare and somehow useful-looking, like a large broom closet. I wondered where they hatched the Protestant plots Cousin Gaston often mentioned, such as the crushing of Mediterranean culture by peaceful means. I remember that I felt lonely and out of place, and took Arnaud's hand. He was wearing his distant, listening-to-music expression, and seemed not to notice. At any rate, he didn't mind.)

Families such as the Ponses had left the area long before, but Arnaud's father said his belongings were too ancient and precious to be bumped down a winding staircase and heaved aboard a van. Papa thought he just wanted to hang on to his renewable lease, which happened to fall under the grace of a haphazard rent-control law: he still paid just about the same rent he had been paying before the war. Whatever he saved had never been squandered on paint or new curtains. His eleven rooms shared the same degree of decay and looked alike: you never knew if you were in a dining room or somebody's bedroom. There were antique tables and bedsteads everywhere. All the mirrors were stained with those dark blotches that resemble maps. Papa often wondered if the Ponses knew what they really looked like, if they actually saw themselves as silvery-white, with parts of their faces spotted or missing.

One of the first things Mme. Pons had ever shown me was a mute harpsichord, which she wanted to pass on to Arnaud and me. To get it to look right—never mind the sound—would have required months of expert mending, more than Arnaud could afford. Looking around for something else to talk about, I saw in a far, dim corner a bathtub and washstand, valuable relics, in their way, streaked and stained with age. Someone had used them recently: the towels on a rack nearby looked damp. I had good reason for thinking the family all used the same towels.

What went wrong for M. Pons, the winter of my engagement? Even Papa never managed to find out. He supposed M. Pons had been giving too much taxation advice, on too grand a scale. He took down from his front door the brass plate mentioning office hours and went to work in a firm that did not carry his name. His wife had an uncommon past, at once aristocratic and vaguely bohemian. My parents wondered what it could mean. My children would inherit a quarter share of blue blood, true, but they might also come by a tendency to dance naked in Montmartre. Her father had been killed in the First World War, leaving furniture, a name, and a long tradition of perishing in battle. She was the first woman in her circle ever to work. Her mother used to cry every morning as she watched her pinning her hat on and counting her lunch money. Her name was Marie-Eugénie-Paule-Diane. Her husband called her Nenanne—I never knew why.

Arnaud had studied law, for the sake of family tradition, but his true calling was to write opinions about music. He wished he had been a music critic on a daily newspaper, incorruptible and feared. He wanted to expose the sham and vulgarity of Paris taste; so he said. Conductors and sopranos would feel the extra edge of anxiety that makes for a good performance, knowing the incorruptible Arnaud Pons was in the house. (Arnaud had no way of judging whether he was incorruptible, my father said. He had never tried earning a living by writing criticism in Paris.)

We spent most of our time together listening to records, while Arnaud told me what was wrong with Toscanini or Bruno Walter. He would stop the record and play the same part again, pointing out the mistakes. The music seemed as worn and shabby as the room. I imagined the musicians in those great orchestras of the past to be covered with dust, playing on instruments cracked, split, daubed with fingerprints, held together with glue and string. My children in Lille had spotless instruments, perfectly tuned. Their music floated into a dark garden drenched with silent rain. But then my thoughts would be overtaken by the yells and screams of one of Arnaud's doomed sopranos—a Tosca, a Mimi—and I would shut my eyes and let myself fall. A still surface of water rose to meet me. I was not dying but letting go.

Bernard's father answered Papa's second approach, which had been much like the first. He said that his son was a student, with no roof or income of his own. It would be a long time before he could join his destiny to anyone's, and it would not be to mine. Bernard had no inclination for me; none whatever. He had taken me to be an attractive and artistic girl, anxious to please, perhaps a bit lonely. As an ardent writer of letters, with pen friends as far away as Belgium, Bernard had offered the hand of epistolary comradeship. I had grabbed the hand and called it a commitment. Bernard was ready to swear in court (should a lawsuit be among my father's insane intentions) that he had taken no risks and never dropped his guard with an unclaimed young person, encountered in a public park. (My parents were puzzled by "unclaimed." I had to explain that I used to take off my engagement ring and carry it loose in a pocket. They asked why. I could not remember.)

M. Brunelle, the answer went on, hoped M. Castelli would put a stop to my fervent outpourings in the form of letters. Their agitated content and their frequency—as many as three a day— interfered with Bernard's studies and, indeed, kept him from sleeping. Surely my father did not want to see me waste the passion of a young heart on a delusion that led nowhere ("on a chimera that can only run dry in the Sahara of disappointment"

90

was what M. Brunelle actually wrote). He begged my father to accept the word of a gentleman that my effusions had been destroyed. "Gentleman" was in English and underlined.

My parents shut themselves up in their bedroom. From my own room, where I sat at the window, holding Bernard's messages, I could hear my father's shouts. He was blaming Maman. Eventually she came in, and I stood up and handed her the whole packet: three letters and a postcard.

"Just the important one," she said. "The one I should have made you show me last April. I want the letter that mentions marriage."

"It was between the lines," I said, watching her face as she read.

"It was nowhere." She seemed sorry for me, all at once. "Oh, Sylvie, Sylvie. My poor Sylvie. Tear it up. Tear every one of them up. All this because you would not try to love Arnaud."

"I thought he loved me," I said. "Bernard, I mean. He never said he didn't."

The Heaven-sent vision of my future life had already faded: the voices of my angelic children became indistinct. I might, now, have been turning the pages of an old storybook with black-and-white engravings.

I said, "I'll apologize to Papa and ask him to forgive me. I can't explain what happened. I thought he wanted what I wanted. He never said that he didn't. I promise never to paint pictures again."

I had not intended the remark about painting pictures. It said itself. Before I could take it back, Maman said, "Forgive you? You're like a little child. Does forgiveness include sending our most humble excuses to the Brunelle family and our having to explain that our only daughter is a fool? Does it account for behavior no sane person can understand? Parents knew what they were doing when they kept their daughters on a short lead. My mother read every letter I wrote until I was married. We were too loving, too lenient."

Her face looked pinched and shrunken. Her love, her loyalties, whatever was left of her youth and charm pulled away from me to be mustered in favor of Papa. She stood perfectly still, almost at attention. I think we both felt at a loss. I thought she was waiting for a signal so she could leave the room. Finally, my father called her. I heard her mutter, "Please get out of my way," though I was nowhere near the door.

My friend Chantal—my postal station, my go-between—came over as soon as she heard the news. It had been whispered by my mother to Chantal's mother, over the telephone, in a version of events that absolved me entirely and turned the Brunelles into fortune-hunting, come-lately provincial merchants and rogues. Chantal knew better, though she still believed the Brunelles had misrepresented their case and came in for censure. She had brought chocolates to cheer me up; we ate most of a box, sitting in a corner of the salon like two travellers in a hotel lobby. She wore her hair in the newest style, cut short and curled thickly on her forehead. I have forgotten the name of the actress who started the fashion: Chantal told me, but I could not take it in.

Chantal was a good friend, perhaps because she had never taken me seriously as a rival; and perhaps in saying this I misjudge her. At any rate, she lost no time in giving me brisk advice. I ought to cut my hair, change my appearance. It was the first step on the way to a new life. She knew I loved children and might never have any of my own: I had no idea how to go about meeting a man or how to hang on to one if he drifted my way. As the next-best thing, I should enter a training college and learn to teach nursery classes. There wasn't much to it, she said. You encouraged them to draw with crayons and sing and run in circles. You put them on pots after lunch and spread blankets on the floor for their afternoon nap. She knew plenty of girls who had done this after their engagements, for some reason, collapsed.

She had recently got to know a naval lieutenant while on a

family holiday in the Alps, and now they were planning a Christmas wedding. Perhaps I could persuade my family to try the
same thing; but finding a fiancé in the mountains was a new
idea—to my mother chancy and doubtful, while my father imagined swindlers and foreigners trampling snow in pursuit of other
men's daughters.

Since the fiasco, as he called it, Papa would not look at me.
When he had anything to say he shouted it to Maman. They did
not take their annual holiday that year but remained in the
shuttered apartment, doing penance for my sins. The whole
world was away, except us. From Normandy, Claudine sent my
mother a postcard of the basilica at Lisieux and the message "My
maman, being a mother, respectfully shares your grief"—as if I
had died.

At dinner one night—curtains drawn, no one saying much—
Papa suddenly held up his hands, palms out. "How many hands
do you count?" he said, straight to me.

"Two?" I made it a question in case it was a trick.

"Right. Two hands. All I needed to pull me to the top of my
profession. I gave my wife the life she wanted, and I gave my
daughter a royal upbringing."

I could sense my mother's close attention, her wanting me to
say whatever Papa expected. He had drunk most of a bottle of
Brouilly by himself and seemed bound for headlong action. In
the end, his message was a simple one: he had forgiven me. My
life was a shambles and our family's reputation gravely injured,
but I was not wholly to blame. Look at the young men I'd had
to deal with: neutered puppies. No wonder there were so many
old maids now. I had missed out on the only virile generation of
the twentieth century, the age group that took in M. Pons,
Cousin Gaston, and, of course, Papa himself.

"We were a strong rung on the ladder of progress," he said.
"After us, the whole ladder broke down." The name of Pons,
seldom mentioned, seemed to evoke some faraway catastrophe,
recalled by a constant few. He bent his head and I thought,

Surely he isn't going to cry. I recalled how my mother had said, "We were too loving." I saw the storehouse in Nice and our name in faded blue. There were no more Castellis, except Julien in Indochina. I put my napkin over my face and began to bawl.

Papa cheered up. "Two hands," he said, this time to Maman. "And no help from any quarter. Isn't that true?"

"Everybody admired you," she said. She was clearing plates, fetching dessert. I was too overcome to help; besides, she didn't want me. She missed Claudine. My mother sat down again and looked at Papa, leaving me out. I was a dreary guest, like Mme. Pons getting ready to show hysteria at the sight of a veal chop. They might have preferred her company to mine, given the choice. She had done them no harm and gave them reasons to laugh. I refused dessert, though no one cared. They continued to eat their fresh figs poached in honey, with double cream: too sugary for Maman, really, but a great favorite of Papa's. "The sweeter the food, the better the temper" was a general truth she applied to married life.

My mother dreamed she saw a young woman pushed off the top of a tall building. The woman plunged head first, with her wedding veil streaming. The veil materialized the next day, as details of the dream returned. At first Maman described the victim as a man, but the veil confirmed her mistake. She mentioned her shock and horror at my remark on the bridge. The dream surely had been sent as a reminder: I was not to be crossed or harshly contradicted or thrust in the wrong direction. Chantal's plans for my future had struck her as worse than foolery: they seemed downright dangerous. I knew nothing about little children. I would let them swallow coins and crayon stubs, leave a child or two behind on our excursions to parks and squares, lose their rain boots and sweaters. Nursery schools were places for nuns and devoted celibates. More to the point, there were no men to be found on the premises, save the occasional inspector, already

94

married, and underpaid. Men earning pittance salaries always married young. It was not an opinion, my mother said. It was a statistic.

Because of the dream she began to show her feelings through hints and silences or by telling anecdotes concerning wretched and despairing spinster teachers she had known. I had never heard their names before and wondered when she had come across all those Martines and Georgettes. My father, closed to dreams, in particular the threatening kind, wanted to know why I felt such an urge to wipe the noses and bottoms of children who were no relation of mine. Dealing with one's own offspring was thankless enough. He spoke of the violent selfishness of the young, their mindless questions, their love of dirt. Nothing was more deadening to an adult intellect than a child's cycle of self-centered days and long, shapeless summers.

I began to sleep late. Nothing dragged me awake, not even the sound of Papa calling my mother from room to room. At noon I trailed unwashed to the kitchen and heated leftover coffee. Claudine, having returned to claim all my mother's attention, rinsed lettuce and breaded cutlets for lunch, and walked around me as though I were furniture. One morning Maman brought my breakfast on a tray, sat down on the edge of the bed, and said Julien had been reported missing. He could be a prisoner or he might be dead. Waiting for news, I was to lead a quiet life and to pray. She was dressed to go out, I remember, wearing clothes for the wrong season—all in pale blue, with a bandeau of forget-me-nots and her turquoise earrings and a number of little chains. Her new watch, Papa's latest present, was the size of a coin. She had to bring it up to her eyes.

"It isn't too late, you know," she said. I stared at her. "Too late for Arnaud."

I supposed she meant he could still be killed in Indochina, if he wanted that. To hear Cousin Gaston and Papa, one could imagine it was all any younger man craved. I started to say that Arnaud was twenty-seven now and might be too old for wars, but Maman broke in: Arnaud had left for Paris and gone to live in Rennes. Last April, after the meeting in the parlor, he had asked his maritime-insurance firm to move him to a branch office. It had taken months to find him the right place; being Arnaud, he wanted not only a transfer but a promotion. Until just five days ago he had never been on his own. There had always been a woman to take care of him; namely, Mme. Pons. Mme. Pons was sure he had already started looking around in Rennes for someone to marry. He would begin with the girls in his new office, probably, and widen the circle to church and concerts.

"It isn't too late," said Maman.

"Arnaud hates me now," I said. "Besides, I can work. I can take a course in something. Mme. Pons worked."

"We don't know what Mme. Pons did."

"I could mind children, take them for walks in the afternoon."

My double file of charges, hand in hand, stopped at the curb. A policeman held up traffic. We crossed and entered the court of an ancient abbey, now a museum. The children clambered over fragments of statues and broken columns. I showed them medieval angels.

Mme. Pons did not want a strange daughter-in-law from a provincial city, my mother said. She wanted me, as before.

For the first time I understood about the compact of mothers and the conspiracy that never ends. They stand together like trees, shadowing and protecting, shutting out the view if it happens to suit them, letting in just so much light. She started to remove the tray, though I hadn't touched a thing.

"Get up, Sylvie," she said. It would have seemed like an order except for the tone. Her coaxing, teasing manner had come back. I was still wondering about the pale-blue dress: was she pretending it was spring, trying to pick up whatever had been dropped in April? "It's time you had your hair cut. Sometimes you look eighteen. It may be part of your trouble. We can lunch at the

Trois Quartiers and buy you some clothes. We're lucky to have Papa. He never grumbles about spending.''

My mother had never had her own bank account or signed a check. As a married woman she would have needed Papa's consent, and he preferred to hand over wads of cash, on demand. Melle Coutard got the envelopes ready and jotted the amounts in a ledger. Owing to a system invented by M. Pons, the money was deducted from Papa's income tax.

"And then," said Maman, "you can go to the mountains for two weeks." It was no surprise: Chantal and her lieutenant wanted to return to Chamonix on a lovers' pilgrimage, but General Nauzan, Chantal's father, would not hear of it unless I went, too. It was part of my mission to sleep in her room: the Nauzans would not have to rush the wedding or have a large and healthy baby appear seven months after the ceremony, to be passed off as premature. So I would not feel like an odd number—in the daytime, that is—the lieutenant would bring along his brother, a junior tennis champion, aged fifteen.

(We were well into our first week at Chamonix before Chantal began to disappear in the afternoon, leaving me to take a tennis lesson from the champion. I think I have a recollection of her telling me, late at night, in the darkness of our shared room, "To tell you the truth, I could do without all that side of it. Do you want to go with him tomorrow, instead of me? He thinks you're very nice." But that kind of remembering is like trying to read a book with some of the pages torn out. Things are said at intervals and nothing connects.)

I got up and dressed, as my mother wanted, and we took the bus to her hairdresser's. She called herself Ingrid. Pasted to the big wall mirror were about a dozen photographs cut from *Paris Match* of Ingrid Bergman and her little boy. I put on a pink smock that covered my clothes and Ingrid cut my long hair. My mother saved a few locks, one for Papa, the others in case I ever wanted to see what I had once been like, later on. The two women decided I would look silly with curls on my forehead, so Ingrid combed the new style sleek.

What Chantal had said was true: I looked entirely different. I seemed poised, sharp, rather daunting. Ingrid held a looking glass up so I could see the back of my head and my profile. I turned my head slowly. I had a slim neck and perfect ears and my mother's forehead. For a second a thought flared, and then it died: with her blue frock and blue floral hat and numerous trinkets Maman was like a little girl dressed up. I stared and stared, and the women smiled at each other. I saw their eyes meet in the mirror. They thought they were watching emerging pride, the kind that could make me strong. Even vanity would have pleased them; any awakening would do.

I felt nothing but the desire for a life to match my changed appearance. It was a longing more passionate and mysterious than any sort of love. My role could not be played by another person. All I had to do now was wait for my true life to reveal itself and the other players to let me in.

My father took the news from Indochina to be part of a family curse. He had hoped I would marry Julien. He would have had Castelli grandchildren. But Julien and I were too close in age and forever squabbling. He was more like a brother. "Lover" still held a small quantity of false knowledge. Perhaps I had always wanted a stranger. Papa said the best were being taken, as in all wars. He was sorry he had not been gunned down in the last one. He was forty-nine and had survived to see his only daughter washed up, a decent family nearly extinct, the whole nation idle and soft.

He repeated all these things, and more, as he drove me to the railway station where I was to meet Chantal, the lieutenant, and the junior champion. His parting words reproached me for indifference to Julien's fate, and I got on the train in tears.

My mother was home, at the neat little desk where she plotted so many grave events. For the first time in her life, she delivered an invitation to dinner by telephone. I still have the letter she sent me in Chamonix, describing what they had had to eat and what Mme. Pons had worn: salmon-pink, sleeveless, with spike heels and fake pearls. She had also worn my rejected engagement ring. Mme. Pons could get away with lack of judgment and taste, now. We were the suppliants.

My father had been warned it would be fish, because of Mme. Pons, but he forgot and said quite loudly, "Are you trying to tell me there's nothing after the turbot? Are the butchers on strike? Is it Good Friday? Has the whole world gone crazy? Poor France!" he said, turning to M. Pons. "I mean it. These changes in manners and customs are part of the decline."

The two guests pretended not to hear. They gazed at my painting of the harbor at Naples—afraid, Papa said later, we might try to give it to them.


When Papa asked if I'd enjoyed myself in the Alps I said, "There was a lot of tennis." It had the dampening effect I had hoped for, and he began to talk about a man who had just deserted from the Army because he was a pacifist, and who ought to be shot. Maman took me aside as soon as she could and told me her news: Arnaud was still undecided. His continued license to choose was like a spell of restless weather. The two mothers studied the sky. How long could it last? He never mentioned me, but Mme. Pons was sure he was waiting for a move.

"What move?" I said. "A letter from Papa?"

"You can't expect Papa to write any more letters," she said. "It has to come from you."

Once again, I let my mother dictate a letter for Arnaud. I had no idea what to say; or, rather, of the correct way of saying anything. It was a formal request for an appointment, at Arnaud's convenience, at the venue of his choice. That was all. I signed my full name: Sylvie Mireille Castelli. I had never written to anyone in Rennes before. I could not imagine his street. I wondered if he lived in someone else's house or had found his own apartment. I wondered who made his breakfast and hung up his clothes and changed the towels in the bathroom. I wondered how he would feel when he saw my handwriting; if he would burn the letter, unread.

He waited ten days before saying he did not mind seeing me, and suggested having lunch in a restaurant. He could come to Paris on a Sunday, returning to Rennes the same day. It seemed to me an enormous feat of endurance. The fastest train, in those days, took more than three hours. He said he would let me know more on the matter very soon. The move to Rennes had worn him down and he needed a holiday. He signed "A. Pons." ("That's new," my father said, about the invitation to lunch. He considered Arnaud's approach to money to be conservative, not to say nervous.)


He arrived in Paris on the third Sunday in October, finally, almost a year to the day from our first meeting. I puzzled over the timetable, wondering why he had chosen to get up at dawn to catch a train that stopped everywhere when there was a direct train two hours later. Papa pointed out the extra-fare sign for the express. "And Arnaud . . ." he said, but left it at that.

Papa and I drove to the old Montparnasse station, where the trains came in from the west of France. Hardly anyone remembers it now: a low gray building with a wooden floor. I have a black-and-white postcard that shows the curb where my father parked his Citroën and the station clock we watched and the door I went through to meet Arnaud face to face. We got there early and sat in the car, holding hands sometimes, listening to a Sunday-morning program of political satire—songs and poems and imitations of men in power—but Papa soon grew tired of laughing alone and switched it off. He smoked four Gitanes from a pack Uncle Gaston had left behind. When his lighter balked he pretended to throw it away, trying to make me smile. I could see nothing funny about the loss of a beautiful silver lighter, the gift of a patient. It seemed wasteful, not amusing. I ate some expensive chocolates I found in the glove compartment: Melle Coutard's, I think.

He kept leaning forward to read the station clock, in case his watch and my watch and the dashboard clock were slow. When it was time, he kissed me and made me promise to call the minute I knew the time of Arnaud's return train, so he could come and fetch me. He gave me the names of two or three restaurants he liked, pointing in the direction of the Boulevard Raspail—places he had taken me that smelled of cigars and red Burgundy. They looked a bit like station buffets, but were more comfortable and far more expensive. I imagined that Arnaud and I would be walking along the boulevard in the opposite direction, where there were plenty of smaller, cheaper places. Papa and Cousin Gaston smoked Gitanes in memory of their student days. They did, sometimes, visit the restaurants of their youth, where the smells were of boiled beef and fried potatoes and dark tobacco, but they knew the difference between a sentimental excursion and a good meal.

As I turned away, my heart pounding enough to shake me, I heard him say, "Remember, whatever happens, you will always have a home," which was true but also a manner of speaking.


The first passenger off the train was a girl with plastic roses pinned to her curly hair. She ran into the arms of two other girls. They looked alike, in the same long coats with ornamental buttons, the same frothy hair and plastic hair slides. One of the Parisians took the passenger's cardboard suitcase and they went off, still embracing and chattering. Chantal had warned me not to speak to any man in the station, even if he seemed respectable. She had described the sad girls who came from the west, a deeply depressed area, to find work as maids and waitresses, and the gangsters who hung around the train gates. They would pick the girls up and after a short time put them on the street. If a girl got tired of the life and tried to run away, they had her murdered and her body thrown in the Seine. The crimes were never solved; nobody cared.

Actually, most of the men I saw looked like citified Breton farmers. I had a problem that seemed, at the moment, far more acute than the possibility of being led astray and forced into prostitution. I had no idea what to say to Arnaud, how to break the ice. My mother had advised me to talk about Rennes if conversation ran thin. I could mention the great fire of 1720 and the fine houses it had destroyed. Arnaud walked straight past me and suddenly turned back. On his arm he carried a new raincoat with a plaid lining. He was wearing gloves; he took one off to shake hands.

I said, "I've had my hair cut."

"So I see."

That put a stop to 1720, or anything else, for the moment. We crossed the Boulevard du Montparnasse without touching or speaking. He turned, as I had expected, in the direction of the cheaper restaurants. We read and discussed the menus posted outside. He settled on Rougeot. Not only did Rougeot have a long artistic and social history, Arnaud said, but it offered a fixed-price meal with a variety of choice. Erik Satie had eaten here. No one guessed how poor Satie had been until after his death, when Cocteau and others had visited his wretched suburban home and learned the truth. Rilke had eaten here, too. It was around the time when he was discovering Cézanne and writing those letters. I recognized Arnaud's way of mentioning famous people, pausing before the name and dropping his voice.

The window tables were already taken. Arnaud made less fuss than I expected. Actually, I had never been alone at a restaurant with Arnaud; it was my father I was thinking of, and how violently he wanted whatever he wanted. Arnaud would not hang up his coat. He had bought it just the day before and did not want a lot of dirty garments full of fleas in close touch. He folded it on a chair, lining out. It fell on the floor every time a waiter went by.

102

I memorized the menu so I could describe it to Maman. Our first course was hard-boiled eggs with mayonnaise, then we chose the liver. Liver was something his mother would not have in the house, said Arnaud. As a result, he and his father were chronically lacking in iron. I wanted to ask where he ate his meals now, if he had an obliging landlady who cooked or if he had the daily expense of a restaurant; but it seemed too much like prying.

The red wine, included in the menu, arrived in a thick, stained decanter. Arnaud asked to be shown the original label. The waiter said the label had been thrown away, along with the bottle. There was something of a sneer in his voice, as if we were foreigners, and Arnaud turned away coldly. The potatoes served with the liver had been boiled early and heated up: we both noticed. Arnaud said it did not matter; because of the wine incident, we were never coming back. "We" suggested a common future, but it may have been a slip of the tongue; I pretended I hadn't heard. For dessert I picked custard flan and Arnaud had prunes in wine. Neither of us was hungry by then, but dessert was included, and it would have been a waste of money to skip a course. Arnaud made some reference to this.

I want to say that I never found him mean. He had not come to Paris to charm or impress me; he was here to test his own feelings at the sight of me and to find out if I understood what getting married meant—in particular, to him. His conversation was calm and instructive. He told me about "situations," meaning the entanglements people got into when they were characters in novels an plays. He compared the theatre of Henry de Montherlant with Jean Anouilh's: how they considered the part played by innocent girls in the lives of more worldly men. To Anouilh a girl was a dove, Arnaud said, an innocent dressed in white, ultimately and almost accidentally destroyed. Montherlant saw them as ignorant rather than innocent—more knowing than any man suspected, unlearned and crass.

All at once he said a personal thing: "You aren't eating your dessert."

"There's something strange on it," I said. "Green flakes."

He pulled my plate over and scraped the top of the flan with my spoon. (I had taken one bite and put the spoon down.) "Parsley," he said. "There was a mistake made in the kitchen. They took the flan for a slice of quiche."

"I know it is paid for," I said. "But I can't."

I was close to tears. It occurred to me that I sounded like Mme. Pons. He began to eat the flan, slowly, using my spoon. Each time he put the spoon in his mouth I said to myself, He must love me. Otherwise it would be disgusting. When he had finished, he folded his napkin in the exact way that always annoyed my mother and said he loved me. Oh, not as before, but enough to let him believe he could live with me. I was not to apologize for last spring or to ask for forgiveness. As Cosima had said to Hans von Bülow, after giving birth to Wagner's child, forgiveness was not called for—just understanding. (I knew who Wagner was, but the rest bewildered me utterly.) I had blurted out something innocent, impulsive, Arnaud continued, and my mother—herself a child—had acted as though it were a mature decision. My mother had told his mother about the bridge and the turning point; he understood that, too. He knew all about infatuation. At one time he had actually believed my drawing of Vesuvius could bring him luck, and had carried it around with the legal papers in his briefcase. That was how eaten up by love he had been, at twenty-six. Well, that kind of storm and passion of the soul was behind him. He was twenty-seven, and through with extremes. He blamed my mother, but one had to take into account her infantile nature. He was inclined to be harder on Bernard—speaking the name easily, as if "Bernard Brunelle" were a character in one of the plays he had just mentioned. Brunelle was a vulgar libertine, toying with the feelings of an untried and trustful girl and discarding her when the novelty wore off. He, Arnaud, was prepared to put the clock back to where it had stood exactly a second before my mother wrenched the wedding invitations out of my hands and hurled them into the Seine.

Seated beside a large window that overlooked the terrace and boulevard were the three curly-haired girls I had noticed at the station. They poured wine for each other and leaned into the table, so that their heads almost touched. Above them floated a flat layer of thin blue smoke. Once I was married, I thought, I would smoke. It would give me something to do with my hands when other people talked, and would make me look as if I were enjoying myself. One of the girls caught me looking, and smiled. It was a smile of recognition, but hesitant, too, as if she wondered if I would want to acknowledge her. She turned back, a little disappointed. When I looked again, I had a glimpse of her in profile, and saw why she had seemed familiar and yet diffident: she was the typist who sat outside Cousin Gaston's office, who had caused Gaston and Papa so much anxiety and apprehension. She was just eighteen—nineteen at most. How could they have taken her for a spy? She was one of three kittenish friends, perhaps sisters, from the poorest part of France.

Look at it this way, Arnaud was saying. We had gone through tests and trials, like Tamino and Pamina, and had emerged tempered and strong. I must have looked blank, for he said, a little sharply, "In *The Magic Flute*. We spent a whole Sunday on it. I translated every word for you—six records, twelve sides."

I said, "Does she die?"

"No," said Arnaud. "If she had to die we would not be sitting here." Now, he said, lowering his voice, there was one more thing he needed to know. This was not low curiosity on his part, but a desire to have the whole truth spread out—"like a sheet spread on green grass, drying in sunshine" was the way he put it. My answer would make no difference; his decisions concerning me and our future were final. The question was, had Bernard Brunelle *succeeded* and, if so, to what extent? Was I entirely, or partly, or not at all the same as before? Again, he said the stranger's name as if it were an invention, a name assigned to an imaginary life.

It took a few moments for me to understand what Arnaud was

talking about. Then I said, "Bernard Brunelle? Why, I've never even kissed him. I saw him only that once. He lives in Lille."

His return train did not leave for another hour. I asked if he would like to walk around Montparnasse and look at the famous cafés my father liked, but the sidewalk was spotted with rain, and I think he did not want to get his coat wet. As we crossed the boulevard again, he took my arm and remarked that he did not care for Bretons and their way of thinking. He would not spend his life in Rennes. Unfortunately, he had asked for the transfer and the firm had actually created a post for him. It would be some time before he could say he had changed his mind. In the meantime, he would come to Paris every other weekend. Perhaps I could come to Rennes, too, with or without a friend. We had reached the age of common sense and could be trusted. Some of the beaches in Brittany were all right, he said, but you never could be sure of the weather. He preferred the Basque coast, where his mother used to take him when he was a child. He had just spent four weeks there, in fact.

I did not dare ask if he had been alone; in any case, he was here, with me. We sat down on a bench in the station. I could think of nothing more to say. The great fire of 1720 seemed inappropriate as a topic for someone who had just declared an aversion to Bretons and their history. I had a headache, and was just as glad to be quiet. I wondered how long it would take to wean him away from the Pons family habit of drinking low-cost wine. He picked up a newspaper someone had left behind and began to read yesterday's news. There was more about the pacifist deserter; traitors (I supposed they must be that) were forming a defense committee. I thought about Basque beaches, wondering if they were sand or shale, and if my children would be able to build sand castles.

Presently Arnaud folded the paper, in the same careful way he always folded a table napkin, and said I ought to follow Chantal's suggestion and get a job teaching in a nursery school. (So Maman had mentioned that to Mme. Pons, too.) I should teach until I had enough working time behind me to claim a pension. It would be good for me in my old age to have an income of my own. Anything could happen. He could be killed in a train crash or called up for a war. My father could easily be ruined in a lawsuit and die covered with debts. There were advantages to teaching, such as long holidays and reduced train fares.

"How long would it take?" I said. "Before I could stop teaching and get my pension."

"Thirty-five years," said Arnaud. "I'll ask my mother. She had no training, either, but she taught private classes. All you need is a decent background and some recommendations."

Wait till Papa hears this, I thought. He had imagined everything possible, even that she had been the paid mistress of a Romanian royal.

Arnaud said a strange thing then: "You would have all summer long for your art. I would never stand in your way. In fact, I would do everything to help. I would mind the children, take them off your hands."

In those days men did not mind children. I had never in my life seen a married man carrying a child except to board a train or at a parade. I was glad my father hadn't heard. I think I was shocked: I believe that, in my mind, Arnaud climbed down a notch. More to the point, I had not touched a brush or drawing pencil since the day my mother had read the letter from Bernard—the important one. Perhaps if I did not paint and draw and get stains on my hands and clothes Arnaud would be disappointed. Perhaps, like Maman, he wanted to be able to say that everything hanging on the walls was mine. What he had said about not standing in my way was unusual, certainly; but it was kind, too.

We stood up and he shook and then folded his coat, holding the newspaper under his arm. He pulled his gloves out of his coat pocket, came to a silent decision, and put them back. He handed me the newspaper, but changed his mind: he would work the crossword puzzle on the way back to Rennes. By the end of the day, I thought, he would have travelled some eight hours and have missed a Sunday-afternoon concert, because of me. He started to say goodbye at the gate, but I wanted to see him board the train. A special platform ticket was required: he hesitated until I said I would buy it myself, and then he bought it for me.

From the step of the train he leaned down to kiss my cheek. I said, "Shall I let it grow back?"

"What?"

"My hair. Do you like it short or long?"

He was unable to answer, and seemed to find the question astonishing. I walked along the platform and saw him enter his compartment. There was a discussion with a lady about the window seat. He would never grab or want anything he had no claim on, but he would always establish his rights, where they existed. He sat down in the place he had a right to, having shown his seat reservation, and opened the paper to the puzzle. I waited until the train pulled away. He did not look out. In his mind I was on my way home.

I was not quite sure what to do next, but I was certain of one thing: I would not call Papa. Arnaud had not called his family, either. We had behaved like a real couple, in a strange city, where we knew no one but each other. From the moment of his arrival until now we had not been separated; not once. I decided I would walk home. It was a long way, much of it uphill once I crossed the river, but I would be moving along, as Arnaud was moving with the train. I would be accompanying him during at least part of his journey.

I began to walk, under a slight, not a soaking, drizzle, along the boulevard, alongside the autumn trees. The gray clouds looked sculptured, the traffic lights unnaturally bright. I was sitting on a sandy beach somewhere along the Basque coast. A red ribbon held my long hair, kept it from blowing across my face. I sat in the shade of a white parasol, upon a striped towel. My knees were drawn up to support my sketch pad. I bent my head and drew my children as they dug holes in the sand. They wore white sun hats. Their arms and legs were brown.

By the time I reached the Invalides the rain had stopped. Instead of taking the shortest route home, I had made a wide detour west. The lights gleamed brighter than ever as night came down. There were yellow streaks low in the sky. I skirted the little park and saw old soldiers, survivors of wars lovingly recalled by Cousin Gaston and Papa, sitting on damp benches. They lived in the veterans' hospital nearby and had nothing else to do. I turned the corner and started down toward the Seine, walking slowly. I still had a considerable distance to cover, but it seemed unfair to arrive home before Arnaud; that was why I had gone so far out of my way. My parents could think whatever they liked: that he had taken a later train, that I had got wet finding a taxi. I would never tell anyone how I had travelled with Arnaud, not even Arnaud. It was a small secret, insignificant, but it belonged to the true life that was almost ready to let me in. And so it did; and, yes, it made me happy.

# FORAIN

About an hour before the funeral service for Adam Tremski, snow mixed with rain began to fall, and by the time the first of the mourners arrived the stone steps of the church were dangerously wet. Blaise Forain, Tremski's French publisher, now his literary executor, was not surprised when, later, an elderly woman slipped and fell and had to be carried by ambulance to the Hôtel-Dieu hospital. Forain, in an attempt to promote Cartesian order over Slavic frenzy, sent for the ambulance, then found himself obliged to accompany the patient to the emergency section and fork over a deposit. The old lady had no social security.

Taken together, façade and steps formed an escarpment—looming, abrupt, above all unfamiliar. The friends of Tremski's last years had been Polish, Jewish, a few French. Of the French, only Forain was used to a variety of last rites. He was expected to attend the funerals not only of his authors but of their wives. He knew all the Polish churches of Paris, the Hungarian mission,

**111**

the synagogues on the Rue Copernic and the Rue de la Victoire, and the mock chapel of the crematorium at Père Lachaise cemetery. For nonbelievers a few words at the graveside sufficed. Their friends said, by way of a greeting, "Another one gone." However, no one they knew ever had been buried from this particular church. The parish was said to be the oldest in the city, yet the edifice built on the ancient site looked forbidding and cold. Tremski for some forty years had occupied the same walkup flat on the fringe of Montparnasse. What was he doing over here, on the wrong side of the Seine?

Four months before this, Forain had been present for the last blessing of Barbara, Tremski's wife, at the Polish church on the Rue Saint-Honoré. The church, a chapel really, was round in shape, with no fixed pews—just rows of chairs pushed together. The dome was a mistake—too imposing for the squat structure—but it had stood for centuries, and only the very nervous could consider it a threat. Here, Forain had noticed, tears came easily, not only for the lost friend but for all the broken ties and old, unwilling journeys. The tears of strangers around him, that is; grief, when it reached him, was pale and dry. He was thirty-eight, divorced, had a daughter of twelve who lived in Nice with her mother and the mother's lover. Only one or two of Forain's friends had ever met the girl. Most people, when told, found it hard to believe he had ever been married. The service for Tremski's wife had been disrupted by the late entrance of *her* daughter—child of her first husband—who had made a show of arriving late, kneeling alone in the aisle, kissing the velvet pall over the coffin, and noisily marching out. Halina was her name. She had straight, graying hair and a cross face with small features. Forain knew that some of the older mourners could remember her as a pretty, unsmiling, not too clever child. A few perhaps thought Tremski was her father and wondered if he had been unkind to his wife. Tremski, sitting with his head bowed, may not have noticed. At any rate, he had never mentioned anything.

112

# Forain

Tremski was Jewish. His wife had been born a Catholic, though no one was certain what had come next. To be blunt, was she in or out? The fact was that she had lived in adultery—if one wanted to be specific—with Tremski until her husband had obliged the pair by dying. There had been no question of a divorce; probably she had never asked for one. For his wedding to Barbara, Tremski had bought a dark-blue suit at a good place, Creed or Lanvin Hommes, which he had on at her funeral, and in which he would be buried. He had never owned another, had shambled around Paris looking as though he slept under restaurant tables, on a bed of cigarette ashes and crumbs. It would have taken a team of devoted women, not just one wife, to keep him spruce.

Forain knew only from hearsay about the wedding ceremony in one of the town halls of Paris (Tremski was still untranslated then, had a job in a bookstore near the Jardin des Plantes, had paid back the advance for the dark-blue suit over eleven months)—the names signed in a register, the daughter's refusal to attend, the wine drunk with friends in a café on the Avenue du Maine. It was a cheerless place, but Tremski knew the owner. He had talked of throwing a party but never got round to it; his flat was too small. Any day now he would move to larger quarters and invite two hundred and fifty intimate friends to a banquet. In the meantime, he stuck to his rented flat, a standard émigré dwelling of the 1950s, almost a period piece now: two rooms on a court, windowless kitchen, splintered floors, unheatable bathroom, no elevator, intimidating landlord—a figure central to his comic anecdotes and private worries. What did his wife think? Nobody knew, though if he had sent two hundred and fifty invitations she would undoubtedly have started to borrow two hundred and fifty glasses and plates. Even after Tremski could afford to move, he remained anchored to his seedy rooms: there were all those books, and the boxes filled with unanswered mail, and the important documents he would not let anyone file. Snapshots and group portraits of novelists and poets, wearing the clothes and haircuts of the fifties and sixties, took up much of a wall. A new desire to sort out the past, put its artifacts in order, had occupied Tremski's conversation on his wedding day. His friends had soon grown bored, although his wife seemed to be listening. Tremski, married at last, was off on an oblique course, preaching the need for discipline and a thought-out future. It didn't last.

At Forain's first meeting with Barbara, they drank harsh tea from mismatched cups and appraised each other in the gray light that filtered in from the court. She asked him, gently, about his fitness to translate and publish Tremski—then still at the bookstore, selling wartime memoirs and paperbacks and addressing parcels. Did Forain have close ties with the Nobel Prize committee? How many of his authors had received important awards, gone on to international fame? She was warm and friendly and made him think of a large buttercup. He was about the age of her daughter, Halina; so Barbara said. He felt paternal, wise, rid of mistaken ideals. He would become Tremski's guide and father. He thought, This is the sort of woman I should have married—although most probably he should never have married anyone.

Only a few of the mourners mounting the treacherous steps can have had a thought to spare for Tremski's private affairs. His wife's flight from a brave and decent husband, dragging by the hand a child of three, belonged to the folklore, not the history, of mid-century emigration. The chronicle of two generations, displaced and dispossessed, had come to a stop. The evaluation could begin; had already started. Scholars who looked dismayingly youthful, speaking the same language, but with a new, jarring vocabulary, were trekking to Western capitals—taping reminiscences, copying old letters. History turned out to be a plodding science. What most émigrés settled for now was the haphazard accuracy of a memory like Tremski's. In the end it was always a poem that ran through the mind—not a string of dates.

# Forain

Some may have wondered why Tremski was entitled to a Christian service; or, to apply another kind of reasoning, why it had been thrust upon him. Given his shifting views on eternity and the afterlife, a simple get-together might have done, with remarks from admirers, a poem or two read aloud, a priest wearing a turtleneck sweater, or a young rabbi with a literary bent. Or one of each, offering prayers and tributes in turn. Tremski had nothing against prayers. He had spent half his life inventing them.

As it turned out, the steep church was not as severe as it looked from the street. It was in the hands of a small charismatic order, perhaps full of high spirits but by no means schismatic. No one had bothered to ask if Tremski was a true convert or just a writer who sometimes sounded like one. His sole relative was his stepdaughter. She had made an arrangement that suited her: she lived nearby, in a street until recently classed as a slum, now renovated and highly prized. Between her seventeenth-century flat and the venerable site was a large, comfortable, cluttered department store, where, over the years, Tremski's friends had bought their pots of paint and rollers, their sturdy plates and cups, their burglarproof door locks, their long-lasting cardigan sweaters. The store was more familiar than the church. The stepdaughter was a stranger.

She was also Tremski's heir and she did not understand Forain's role, taking executor to mean an honorary function, godfather to the dead. She had told Forain that Tremski had destroyed her father and blighted her childhood. He had enslaved her mother, spoken loud Polish in restaurants, had tried to keep Halina from achieving a French social identity. Made responsible, by his astonishing will, for organizing a suitable funeral, she had chosen a French send-off, to be followed by burial in a Polish cemetery outside Paris. Because of the weather and because there was a shortage of cars, friends were excused from attending the burial. Most of them were thankful: more than one fatal cold had been brought on by standing in the icy mud of a graveyard. When she had complained she was doing her best, that Tremski

**115**

had never said what he wanted, she was probably speaking the truth. He could claim one thing and its opposite in the same sentence. Only God could keep track. If today's rite was a cosmic error, Forain decided, it was up to Him to erase Tremski's name from the ledger and enter it in the proper column. If He cared.

The mourners climbed the church steps slowly. Some were helped by younger relatives, who had taken time off from work. A few had migrated to high-rise apartments in the outer suburbs, to deeper loneliness but cheaper rents. They had set out early, as if they still believed no day could start without them, and after a long journey underground and a difficult change of direction had emerged from the Hôtel de Ville Métro station. They held their umbrellas at a slant, as if countering some force of nature arriving head-on. Actually, there was not the least stir in the air, although strong winds and sleet were forecast. The snow and rain came down in thin soft strings, clung to fur or woollen hats, and became a meagre amount of slush underfoot.

Forain was just inside the doors, accepting murmured sympathy and handshakes. He was not usurping a family role but trying to make up for the absence of Halina. Perhaps she would stride in late, as at her mother's funeral, driving home some private grudge. He had on a long cashmere overcoat, the only black garment he owned. A friend had left it to him. More exactly, the friend, aware that he was to die very soon, had told Forain to collect it at the tailor's. It had been fitted, finished, paid for, never worn. Forain knew there was a mean joke abroad about his wearing dead men's clothes. It also applied to his professional life: he was supposed to have said he preferred the backlist of any dead writer to the stress and tension of trying to deal with a live one.

His hair and shoes felt damp. The hand he gave to be shaken must have chilled all those it touched. He was squarely in the path of one of those church drafts that become gales anywhere close to a door. He wondered if Halina had been put off coming

116

because of some firm remarks of his, the day before (he had defended Tremski against the charge of shouting in restaurants), or even had decided it was undignified to pretend she cared for a second how Tremski was dispatched; but at the last minute she turned up, with her French husband—a reporter of French political affairs on a weekly—and a daughter of fourteen in jacket and jeans. These two had not been able to read a word of Tremski's until Forain had published a novel in translation about six years before. Tremski believed they had never looked at it—to be fair, the girl was only eight at the time—or any of the books that had followed; although the girl clipped and saved reviews. It was remarkable, Tremski had said, the way literate people, reasonably well travelled and educated, comfortably off, could live adequate lives without wanting to know what had gone before or happened elsewhere. Even the husband, the political journalist, was like that: a few names, a date looked up, a notion of geography satisfied him.

Forain could tell Tremski minded. He had wanted Halina to think well of him at least on one count, his life's work. She was the daughter of a former Army officer who had died—like Barbara, like Tremski—in a foreign city. She considered herself, no less than her father, the victim of a selfish adventure. She also believed she was made of better stuff than Tremski, by descent and status, and that was harder to take. In Tremski's own view, comparisons were not up for debate.

For the moment, the three were behaving well. It was as much as Forain expected from anybody. He had given up measuring social conduct, except where it ran its course in fiction. His firm made a specialty of translating and publishing work from Eastern and Central Europe; it kept him at a remove. Halina seemed tamed now, even thanked him for standing in and welcoming all those strangers. She had a story to explain why she was late, but it was farfetched, and Forain forgot it immediately. The delay most likely had been caused by a knockdown argument over the jacket and jeans. Halina was a cold skirmisher, narrow in scope but heavily principled. She wore a fur-and-leather coat, a pale gray hat with a brim, and a scarf—authentic Hermès? Taiwan fake? Forain could have told by rubbing the silk between his fingers, but it was a wild idea, and he kept his distance.

The girl had about her a look of Barbara: for that reason, no other, Forain found her appealing. Blaise ought to sit with the family, she said—using his first name, the way young people did now. A front pew had been kept just for the three of them. There was plenty of room. Forain thought that Halina might begin to wrangle, in whispers, within earshot (so to speak) of the dead. He said yes, which was easier than to refuse, and decided no. He left them at the door, greeting stragglers, and found a place at the end of a pew halfway down the aisle. If Halina mentioned anything, later, he would say he had been afraid he might have to leave before the end. She walked by without noticing and, once settled, did not look around.

The pale hat had belonged to Halina's mother. Forain was sure he remembered it. When his wife died, Tremski had let Halina and her husband ransack the flat. Halina made several trips while the husband waited downstairs. He had come up only to help carry a crate of papers belonging to Tremski. It contained, among other documents, some of them rubbish, a number of manuscripts not quite complete. Since Barbara's funeral Tremski had not bothered to shave or even put his teeth in. He sat in the room she had used, wearing a dressing gown torn at the elbows. Her wardrobe stood empty, the door wide, just a few hangers inside. He clutched Forain by the sleeve and said that Halina had taken some things of his away. As soon as she realized her error she would bring them back.

Forain would have preferred to cross the Seine on horseback, lashing at anyone who resembled Halina or her husband, but he had driven to her street by taxi, past the old, reassuring, unchanging department store. No warning, no telephone call: he walked up a curving stone staircase, newly sandblasted and scrubbed, and pressed the doorbell on a continued note until someone came running.

118

She let him in, just so far. "Adam can't be trusted to look after his own affairs," she said. "He was always careless and dirty, but now the place smells of dirt. Did you look at the kitchen table? He must keep eating from the same plate. As for my mother's letters, if that's what you're after, he had already started to tear them up."

"Did you save any?"

"They belong to me."

How like a ferret she looked, just then; and she was the child of such handsome parents. A studio portrait of her father, the Polish officer, taken in London, in civilian clothes, smoking a long cigarette, stood on a table in the entrance hall. (Forain was admitted no further.) Forain took in the likeness of the man who had fought a war for nothing. Barbara had deserted that composed, distinguished, somewhat careful face for Tremski. She must have forced Tremski's hand, arrived on his doorstep, bag, baggage, and child. He had never come to a resolution about anything in his life.

Forain had retrieved every scrap of paper, of course—all but the letters. Fired by a mixture of duty and self-interest, he was unbeatable. Halina had nothing on her side but a desire to reclaim her mother, remove the Tremski influence, return her—if only her shoes and blouses and skirts—to the patient and defeated man with his frozen cigarette. Her entitlement seemed to include a portion of Tremski, too; but she had resented him, which weakened her grasp. Replaying every move, Forain saw how strong her case might have been if she had acknowledged Tremski as her mother's choice. Denying it, she became—almost became; Forain stopped her in time—the defendant in a cheap sort of litigation.

Tremski's friends sat with their shoes in puddles. They kept their gloves on and pulled their knitted scarves tight. Some had spent all these years in France without social security or health insurance, either for want of means or because they had never found their feet in the right sort of employment. Possibly they believed that a long life was in itself full payment for a safe old age. Should the end turn out to be costly and prolonged, then, please, allow us to dream and float in the thickest, deepest darkness, unaware of the inconvenience and clerical work we may cause. So, Forain guessed, ran their prayers.

Funerals came along in close ranks now, especially in bronchial winters. One of Forain's earliest recollections was the Mass in Latin, but he could not say he missed it: he associated Latin with early-morning hunger, and sitting still. The charismatic movement seemed to have replaced incomprehension and mystery with theatricals. He observed the five priests in full regalia sitting to the right of the altar. One had a bad cold and kept taking a handkerchief from his sleeve. Another more than once glanced at his watch. A choir, concealed or on tape, sang "Jesu, bleibet meine Freude," after which a smooth trained voice began to recite the Twenty-fifth Psalm. The voice seemed to emanate from Tremski's coffin but was too perfectly French to be his. In the middle of Verse 7, just after "Remember not the sins of my youth," the speaker wavered and broke off. A man seated in front of Forain got up and walked down the aisle, in a solemn and ponderous way. The coffin was on a trestle, draped in purple and white, heaped with roses, tulips, and chrysanthemums. He edged past it, picked up a black box lying on the ground, and pressed two clicking buttons. "Jesu" started up, from the beginning. Returning, the stranger gave Forain an angry stare, as if he had created the mishap.

Forain knew that some of Tremski's friends thought he was unreliable. He had a reputation for not paying authors their due. There were writers who complained they had never received the price of a postage stamp; they could not make sense of his elegant handwritten statements. Actually, Tremski had been the exception. Forain had arranged his foreign rights, when they began to occur, on a half-and-half basis. Tremski thought of money as a useful substance that covered rent and cigarettes. His wife didn't see it that way. Her forefinger at the end of a column of figures, her quiet, seductive voice saying, "Blaise, what's this?" called for a thought-out answer.

She had never bothered to visit Forain's office, but made him take her to tea at Angelina's, on the Rue de Rivoli. After her strawberry tart had been eaten and the plate removed, she would bring out of her handbag the folded, annotated account. Outdone, outclassed, slipping the tearoom check into his wallet to be dissolved in general expenses, he would look around and obtain at least one satisfaction: she was still the best-looking woman in sight, of any age. He had not been tripped up by someone of inferior appearance and quality. The more he felt harassed by larger issues, the more he made much of small compensations. He ran his business with a staff of loyal, worn-out women, connected to him by a belief in what he was doing, or some lapsed personal tie, or because it was too late and they had nowhere to go. At eight o'clock this morning, the day of the funeral, his staunch Lisette, at his side from the beginning of the venture, had called to tell him she had enough social-security points for retirement. He saw the points as splashes of ink on a clean page. All he could think to answer was that she would soon get bored, having no reason to get up each day. Lisette had replied, not disagreeably, that she planned to spend the next ten years in bed. He could not even coax her to stay by improving her salary: except for the reserve of capital required by law, he had next to no money, had to scrape to pay the monthly settlement on his daughter, and was in continual debt to printers and banks.

He was often described in the trade as poor but selfless. He had performed an immeasurable service to world culture, bringing to the West voices that had been muffled for decades in the East. Well, of course, his thimble-size firm had not been able to attract the leviathan prophets, the booming novelists, the great mentors and tireless definers. Tremski had been at the very limit of Forain's financial reach—good Tremski, who had stuck to

Forain even after he could have moved on. Common sense had kept Forain from approaching the next-best, second-level oracles, articulate and attractive, subsidized to the ears, chain-smoking and explaining, still wandering the universities and congresses of the West. Their travel requirements were beyond him: no grant could cover the unassuming but ruinous little hotel on the Left Bank, the long afternoons and evenings spent in bars with leather armchairs, where the visitors expected to meet clever and cultivated people in order to exchange ideas.

Forain's own little flock, by contrast, seemed to have entered the world with no expectations. Apart from the odd, rare, humble complaint, they were content to be put up on the top story of a hotel with a steep, neglected staircase, a wealth of literary associations, and one bath to a floor. For recreation, they went to the café across the street, made a pot of hot water and a tea bag last two and a half hours, and, as Forain encouraged them to keep in mind, could watch the Market Economy saunter by. Docile, holding only a modest estimation of their own gifts, they still provided a handicap: their names, like those of their characters, all sounded alike to barbaric Western ears. It had been a triumph of perseverance on the part of Forain to get notice taken of their books. He wanted every work he published to survive in collective memory, even when the paper it was printed on had been pulped, burned in the city's vast incinerators or lay moldering at the bottom of the Seine.

Season after season, his stomach eaten up with anxiety, his heart pounding out hope, hope, hope, he produced a satirical novella set in Odessa; a dense, sober private journal, translated from the Romanian, best understood by the author and his friends; or another wry glance at the harebrained makers of history. (There were few women. In that particular part of Europe they seemed to figure as brusque flirtatious mistresses or uncomplaining wives.) At least once a year he committed the near-suicide of short stories and poetry. There were rewards, none financial. A few critics thought it a safe bet occasionally to

122

mention a book he sent along for review: he was considered sound in an area no one knew much about, and too hard up to sponsor a pure disaster. Any day now some stumbling tender newborn calf of his could turn into a literary water ox. As a result, it was not unusual for one of his writers to receive a sheaf of tiny clippings, sometimes even illustrated by a miniature photograph, taken at the Place de la Bastille, with traffic whirling around. A clutch of large banknotes would have been good, too, but only Tremski's wife had held out for both.

Money! Forain's opinion was the same as that of any poet striving to be read in translation. He never said so. The name of the firm, Blaise Editions, rang with an honest chime in spheres where trade and literature are supposed to have no connection. When the Minister of Culture had decorated him, not long before, mentioning in encouraging terms Forain's addition to the House of Europe, Forain had tried to look diffident but essential. It seemed to him at that instant that his reputation for voluntary self-denial was a stone memorial pinning him to earth. He wanted to cry out for help—to the Minister? It would look terrible. He felt honored but confused. Again, summoned to the refurbished embassy of a new democracy, welcomed by an ambassador and a cultural attaché recently arrived (the working staff was unchanged), Forain had dared say to himself, "Why don't they just give me the check for whatever all this is costing?"—the champagne, the exquisite catering, the medal in a velvet box—all the while hoping his thoughts would not show on his face.

The truth was that the destruction of the Wall—radiant paradigm—had all but demolished Forain. The difference was that Forain could not be hammered to still smaller pieces and sold all over the world. In much the same way Vatican II had reduced to bankruptcy more than one publisher of prayer books in Latin. A couple of them had tried to recoup by dumping the obsolete missals on congregations in Asia and Africa, but by the time the Third World began to ask for its money back the publishers had gone down with all hands. Briefly, Forain pondered the possibility of unloading on readers in Senegal and Cameroon the entire edition of a subtle and allusive study of corruption in Minsk, set in 1973. Could one still get away with it—better yet, charge it off to cultural coöperation? He answered himself: No. Not after November 1989. Gone were the stories in which socialist incoherence was matched by Western irrelevance. Gone from Forain's intention to publish, that is: his flock continued to turn them in. He had instructed his underpaid, patient professional readers—teachers of foreign languages, for the most part—to look only at the first three and last two pages of any manuscript. If they promised another version of the East-West dilemma, disguised as a fresh look at the recent past, he did not want to see so much as a one-sentence summary.

By leaning into the aisle he could watch the last blessing. A line of mourners, Halina and her sobbing daughter at the head, shuffled around the coffin, each person ready to add an individual appeal for God's mercy. Forain stayed where he was. He neither pestered nor tried to influence imponderables; not since the death of the friend who had owned the cashmere coat. If the firm went into deeper decline, if it took the slide from shaky to foundering, he would turn to writing. Why not? At least he knew what he wanted to publish. It would get rid of any further need of dealing with living authors: their rent, their divorces, their abscessed teeth, not to speak of that new craze in the East—their psychiatrists. His first novel—what would he call it? He allowed a title to rise from his dormant unconscious imagination. It emerged, black and strong, on the cover of a book propped up in a store window: *The Cherry Orchard*. His mind accepted the challenge. What about a sly, quiet novel, teasingly based on the play? A former property owner, after forty-seven years of exile, returns to Karl-Marx-Stadt to reclaim the family home. It now houses sixteen hardworking couples and thirty-eight small children. He throws them out, and the novel winds down with a moody description of curses and fistfights as imported workers try to install a satellite dish in the garden, where the children's swings used to be. It would keep a foot in the old territory, Forain thought, but with a radical shift of focus. He had to move sidelong: he could not all of a sudden start to publish poems about North Sea pollution and the threat to the herring catch.

Here was a joke he could have shared with Tremski. The stepdaughter had disconnected the telephone while Tremski was still in hospital, waiting to die; not that Forain wanted to dial an extinct number and let it ring. Even in Tremski's mortal grief over Barbara, the thought of Forain as his own author would have made him smile. He had accepted Forain, would listen to nothing said against him—just as he could not be dislodged from his fusty apartment and had remained faithful to his wife—but he had considered Forain's best efforts to be a kind of amateur, Western fiddling, and all his bright ideas to be false dawns. Forain lived a publisher's dream life, Tremski believed—head of a platoon of self-effacing, flat-broke writers who asked only to be read, believing they had something to say that was crucial to the West, that might even goad it into action. What sort of action? Forain still wondered. The intelligent fellow whose remains had just been committed to eternity was no different. He knew Forain was poor but believed he was rich. He thought a great new war would leave Central Europe untouched. The liberating missiles would sail across without ruffling the topmost leaf of a poplar tree. As for the contenders, well, perhaps their time was up.

The congregation had risen. Instead of a last prayer, diffuse and anonymous, Forain chose to offer up a firmer reminder of Tremski: the final inventory of his flat. First, the entrance, where a faint light under a blue shade revealed layers of coats on pegs but not the boots and umbrellas over which visitors tripped. Barbara had never interfered, never scolded, never tried to clean things up. It was Tremski's place. Through an archway, the room Barbara had used. In a corner, the chair piled with newspapers and journals that Tremski still intended to read. Next, unpainted shelves containing files, some empty, some spilling foolscap not to be touched until Tremski had a chance to sort everything out. Another bookcase, this time with books. Above it, the spread of photographs of his old friends. A window, and the sort of view that prisoners see. In front of the window, a drop-leaf table that had to be cleared for meals. The narrow couch, still spread with a blanket, where Halina had slept until she ran away. (To the end, Barbara had expected her to return saying, "It was a mistake." Tremski would have made her welcome and even bought another sofa, at the flea market, for the child.) The dark-red armchair in which Forain had sat during his first meeting with Barbara. Her own straight-backed chair and the small desk where she wrote business letters for Tremski. On the wall, a charcoal drawing of Tremski—by an amateur artist, probably—dated June 1945. It was a face that had come through; only just.

Mourners accustomed to the ceremonial turned to a neighbor to exchange the kiss of peace. Those who were not shrank slightly, as if the touch without warmth were a new form of aggression. Forain found unfocussed, symbolized love positively terrifying. He refused the universal coming-together, rammed his hands in his pockets—like a rebellious child—and joined the untidy lines shuffling out into the rain.


Two hours later, the time between amply filled by the accident, the arrival and departure of the ambulance, the long admittance procedure, and the waiting around natural to a service called Emergency, Forain left the hospital. The old lady was too stunned to have much to say for herself, but she could enunciate clearly, "No family, no insurance." He had left his address and, with even less inclination, a check he sincerely hoped was not a dud. The wind and sleet promised earlier in the day battered and drenched him. He skirted the building and, across a narrow street, caught sight of lines of immigrants standing along the north side of central police headquarters. Algerians stood in a separate queue.

There were no taxis. He was too hungry and wet to cross the bridge to the Place Saint-Michel—a three-minute walk. In a café on the Boulevard du Palais he hung his coat where he could keep an eye on it and ordered a toasted ham-and-cheese sandwich, a glass of Badoit mineral water, a small carafe of wine, and black coffee—all at once. The waiter forgot the wine. When he finally remembered, Forain was ready to leave. He wanted to argue about the bill but saw that the waiter looked frightened. He was young, with clumsy hands, feverish red streaks under his eyes, and coarse fair hair: foreign, probably working without papers, in the shadow of the most powerful police in France. All right, Forain said to himself, but no tip. He noticed how the waiter kept glancing toward someone or something at the far end of the room: his employer, Forain guessed. He felt, as he had felt much of the day, baited, badgered, and trapped. He dropped a tip of random coins on the tray and pulled on his coat. The waiter grinned but did not thank him, put the coins in his pocket, and carried the untouched wine back to the kitchen.

Shoulders hunched, collar turned up, Forain made his way to the taxi rank at the Place Saint-Michel. Six or seven people under streaming umbrellas waited along the curb. Around the corner a cab suddenly drew up and a woman got out. Forain took her place, as if it were the most natural thing in the world. He had stopped feeling hungry, but seemed to be wearing layers of damp towels. The driver, in a heavy accent, probably Portuguese, told Forain to quit the taxi. He was not allowed to pick up a passenger at that particular spot, close to a stand. Forain pointed out that the stand was empty. He snapped the lock shut—as if that made a difference—folded his arms, and sat shivering. He wished the driver the worst fate he could think of—to stand on the north side of police headquarters and wait for nothing.

"You're lucky to be working," he suddenly said. "You should

see all those people without jobs, without papers, just over there, across the Seine."

"I've seen them," the driver said. "I could be out of a job just for picking you up. You should be waiting your turn next to that sign, around the corner."

They sat for some seconds without speaking. Forain studied the set of the man's neck and shoulders; it was rigid, tense. An afternoon quiz show on the radio seemed to take his attention, or perhaps he was pretending to listen and trying to decide if it was a good idea to appeal to a policeman. Such an encounter could rebound against the driver, should Forain turn out to be someone important—assistant to the office manager of a Cabinet minister, say.

Forain knew he had won. It was a matter of seconds now. He heard "What was the name of the Queen of Sheba?" "Which one?" "The one who paid a visit to King Solomon." "Can you give me a letter?" "B." "Brigitte?"

The driver moved his head back and forth. His shoulders dropped slightly. Using a low, pleasant voice, Forain gave the address of his office, offering the Saint Vincent de Paul convent as a landmark. He had thought of going straight home and changing his shoes, but catching pneumonia was nothing to the loss of the staunch Lisette; the sooner he could talk to her, the better. She should have come to the funeral. He could start with that. He realized that he had not given a thought to Tremski for almost three hours now. He continued the inventory, his substitute for a prayer. He was not sure where he had broken off—with the telephone on Barbara's desk? Tremski would not have a telephone in the room where he worked, but at the first ring he would call through the wall, "Who is it?" Then "What does he want? . . . He met me *where?* . . . When we were in high school? . . . Tell him I'm too busy. No—let me talk to him."

The driver turned the radio up, then down. "I could have lost my job," he said.

Every light in the city was ablaze in the dark rain. Seen

through rivulets on a window, the least promising streets showed glitter and well-being. It seemed to Forain that in Tremski's dark entry there had been a Charlie Chaplin poster, relic of some Polish film festival. There had been crates and boxes, too, that had never been unpacked. Tremski would not move out, but in a sense he had never moved in. Suddenly, although he had not really forgotten them, Forain remembered the manuscripts he had snatched back from Halina. She had said none was actually finished, but what did she know? What if there were only a little, very little, left to be composed? The first thing to do was have them read by someone competent—not his usual painstaking and very slow professional readers but a bright young Polish critic, who could tell at a glance what was required. Filling gaps was a question of style and logic, and could just as well take place after translation.

When they reached the Rue du Bac the driver drew up as closely as he could to the entrance, even tried to wedge the cab between two parked cars, so that Forain would not have to step into a gutter filled with running water. Forain could not decide what to do about the tip, whether to give the man something extra (it was true that he could have refused to take him anywhere) or make him aware he had been aggressive. "You should be waiting your turn. . . ." still rankled. In the end, he made a Tremski-like gesture, waving aside change that must have amounted to 35 percent of the fare. He asked for a receipt. It was not until after the man had driven away that Forain saw he had not included the tip in the total sum. No Tremski flourish was ever likely to carry a reward. That was another lesson of the day.

More than a year later, Lisette—now working only part-time—mentioned that Halina had neglected to publish in *Le Monde* the anniversary notice of Tremski's death. Did Forain want one to appear, in the name of the firm? Yes, of course. It would be wrong to say he had forgotten the apartment and everything in it, but the inventory, the imaginary camera moving around the rooms, filled him with impatience and a sense of useless effort. His mind stopped at the narrow couch with the brown blanket, Halina's bed, and he said to himself, What a pair those two were. The girl was right to run away. As soon as he had finished the thought he placed his hand over his mouth, as if to prevent the words from emerging. He went one further—bowed his head, like Tremski at Barbara's funeral, promising himself he would keep in mind things as they once were, not as they seemed to him now. But the apartment was vacated, and Tremski had disappeared. He had been prayed over thoroughly by a great number of people, and the only enjoyment he might have had from the present scene was to watch Forain make a fool of himself to no purpose.

There were changes in the office, too. Lisette had agreed to stay for the time it would take to train a new hand: a thin, pretty girl, part of the recent, nonpolitical emigration—wore a short leather skirt, said she did not care about money but loved literature and did not want to waste her life working at something dull. She got on with Halina and had even spared Forain the odd difficult meeting. As she began to get the hang of her new life, she lost no time spreading the story that Forain had been the lover of Barbara and would not let go a handsome and expensive coat that had belonged to Tremski. A posthumous novel-length manuscript of Tremski's was almost ready for the printer, with a last chapter knitted up from fragments he had left trailing. The new girl, gifted in languages, compared the two versions and said he would have approved; and when Forain showed a moment of doubt and hesitation she was able to remind him of how, in the long run, Tremski had never known what he wanted.

# A State of Affairs

O wing to his advanced age and a lack of close relatives, M. Wroblewski receives little personal mail. Most of the friends of his youth in Warsaw are dead and the survivors have not much to say, except about their grandchildren, and one cannot keep writing back and forth about total strangers. Even the grandparents know them only through colored snapshots or as shrill, shy voices over the telephone. They barely say anything in Polish and have English-sounding names: their parents emigrated as soon as they could. M. Wroblewski's wife has a niece in Canberra: Teresa, wife of Stanley, mother of Fiona and Tim. He keeps their photographs filed in large brown envelopes. Should Teresa and her family ever decide to visit Paris, he will spread their cheerful faces all over the flat.

You might imagine that changed conditions in Eastern Europe would stir some hope into the news from Warsaw, but his correspondents, the few who are left, sound dispirited, mistrustful. Everything costs too much. Young people are ignorant and rude. The spoken language is debased. Purses are snatched on church steps. There are no books worth reading—nothing but pornography and translated Western trash. Recently, a friend he has not seen in fifty years but with whom he has kept in touch sent him a long letter. The friend had been invited to describe his wartime ghetto experience in a radio talk. As a result, he was sent messages of insult and abuse. There was even a death threat. He is an old man. Surely enough is enough. "On that score, nothing has changed," he wrote. "It is in the brain, blood, and bone. I don't mean this for you. You were always different."

A compliment, yes, but no one wants to be singled out, tested, examined, decreed an exception. "I don't mean this for you" leads to awkwardness and painful feelings. Perhaps, a long time ago, as a young man, callow and cordial, M. Wroblewski had said the same thing to his friend: "Naturally, you are completely different. I'm talking about all the others." Could he have said it? He would like to be able to send his friend a plane ticket to Paris, find him a comfortable room and discreetly settle the bill, invite him to dinner: M. Wroblewski, his friend, and Magda around the little table in the living room, with the green lamp-shade glowing and the green curtains drawn; or at Chez Marcel, where he used to go with Magda. The owner would remember them, offer free glasses of cognac with their coffee: jovial, gener-ous, welcoming—One Europe, One World.

There, you see, M. Wroblewski would tell his friend. There are chinks of light.

This is a soft autumn, moist and mild. Between showers the broad boulevards fill up with people strolling as though it were summer. He sits in the Atelier, the new place just next door to the Select, composing and rejecting an answer to his friend. His hat and stick are on a chair; his dog, an obedient one, lies under it. The Atelier opened in the eighties, but he still thinks of it as "the new place." It seems to have been in Montparnasse forever. The table mats depict a mature model posing for a life class some three generations ago. Newspapers are on wooden holders, in the old way. The waiters are patient, except when a customer's reaction to a slopped saucer is perceived as an affront. Across the street the mirrored walls of the building that now rises above the Coupole reflect an Île-de-France sky: watered blue with a thin screen of clouds. If you sit at the front row of tables you may be pestered by foreign beggars, some of them children. M. Wroblewski keeps loose change in his pocket, which he distributes until it runs out. There have been many newspaper articles warning him not to do this: the money is collected for the brutal and cynical men who put the children on the street.

His friend in Warsaw is completely alert, with an amazing memory of events, sorted out, in sequence. If he were here, at this moment, he would find a historical context for everything: the new building and its mirrors, the naked model, the beggar girl with her long braid of hair and the speck of diamond on the side of her nose. Who, after hearing the voice of an old man over the radio, could sit down and compose a threat? All M. Wroblewski can see are a man's hunched shoulders, the back of his thick neck. But no, his friend might say: I have seen his face, which is lean and elegant. What do you still hope for? What can you still expect? So much for your chinks of light.

And so they would exchange visions through the afternoon and into the evening, with the lights inside the café growing brighter and brighter as the trees outside become part of the night. Perhaps his friend would enjoy meeting someone wholly new, remote from the dark riddle of the man and the death letter. Unfortunately, most of M. Wroblewski's Paris acquaintances have vanished or moved away to remote towns and suburbs (everything seems far) or retired to a region of the mind that must be like a twisted, hollow shell. When he reads his wife a letter from Canberra he takes care to translate the English expressions Teresa puts in as a matter of course. Magda used to understand English, but even her French is fading now. Before he reaches the end of the letter she will have asked four or five times, "Who is it from?"—although he has shown her the signature and the bright Australian stamps. Or she may surprise him with a pertinent question: "Are they coming home for Christmas?" There is no telling what Magda means by home. She may say to him, "Does my father like you?" or even, "Where do you live?"

She uses his diminutive, says "Maciek and I," but knows nothing about him. She can play a game of cards, write a letter—it is never clear to whom—and he pretends to stamp and post it. By the time he has invented a plausible address, the incident has dissolved. She stares at the envelope. What is he talking about? She is poised on the moment between dark and light, when the last dream of dawn is shredding rapidly and awareness of morning has barely caught hold. She lives that split second all day long.

This morning, when he brought in her breakfast tray, he found a new letter astray on the carpet. Her writing is larger than before, easy to read:

My Dearest Dear!
    Maciek is teaching and so am I! At the Polish high school in Paris! He teaches French. I teach algebra and music. Our pupils are well behaved. We have Nansen passports! They open wide, like an accordion. Only a few lucky people are allowed to have Nansen passports! They are very old! Only a few people can have them. Maciek is teaching French.

                                        Your loving
                                        Magda

Everything in the letter is true, if you imagine that today is unwinding some forty-five years ago. He said, "What a nice letter. Is it for Teresa?"

She sat up in bed, accepted tea. "What is Prussia?"

The Prussia question is new. Perhaps in one of the shredded dreams someone called out "Prussia!" in a dream voice that turned words and names into dramatic affirmations. She looked toward the window, sipped her tea. She could see (if she was taking it in) the big garage at the corner and at least one of the trees on Boulevard Raspail.

"They've cut some trees down," she remarked not long ago, walking with him around the block. She was right: it was he who failed to notice the gaps, even though he goes along the boulevard every day of his life.

Unless you try to keep a conversation alive, nothing shows. When he takes her out in the afternoon for tea and a slice of fruitcake, she looks finer and more self-possessed than most of the old ladies at other tables. They make a mess with crumbs, feed piecrust to their unruly lapdogs, pester the waiter with questions as repetitive and tedious as any of Magda's: Why is that door open? Why doesn't someone shut the door? Well, why can't you get somebody to fix it? The trouble about Magda is only that one can't leave her alone for a minute or she will be out in the street, trying to climb on a bus, on her way to teach a solfège class in a Polish school that no longer exists.

Morning is the slow time, when she refuses to understand the first thing about buttons, zippers, a comb, a toothbrush. Marie-Louise, who was born in Martinique, arrives at nine o'clock, five days a week. She knows how to coax Magda out of bed and into her clothes. (A bath can take three-quarters of an hour.) At last, neatly dressed, holding hands with Marie-Louise, she will watch a program of cartoons or a cooking lesson or a hooded man sticking up an American bank. Still clutching Marie-Louise, she may say, in Polish, "Who is this woman? I don't like this woman. Tell her to go away."

Marie-Louise is sent by the city's social services and costs them nothing. The rules are firm: household tasks are banned, but she may, as a favor, start the washing machine or make a compote of apples and pears for Magda's lunch. In the meantime, he does the shopping, walks the dog. If Marie-Louise says she can stay until noon he walks up to Montparnasse and reads the newspapers. The white awning and umbrellas at the Atelier bring to mind the South, when Nice and Monaco were still within his means and not too crowded. He and Magda went down every Easter, travelling third class. He can retrace every step of their holiday round: beach in the morning, even when Easter fell in March and the sea was too cold for wading; a picnic lunch of bread, cheese, and fruit, eaten in deck chairs along the front; a rest; a long walk, then a change into spotless, pressed clothes—cream and ivory tones for Magda, beige or lightweight navy for him. An apéritif under a white awning; dinner at the pension. (In the dining room the Wroblewskis kept to themselves.) After dinner, a visit to the casino—not to gamble but to watch the most civilized people in Western Europe throw their money around. You would have to be a millionaire to live that way now.

In Montparnasse, the other day, a woman sitting by herself turned on a small radio. The music sounded like early Mozart or late Haydn. No one complained, and so the waiters said nothing. Against the music, he tried to calculate, in sums that have no bearing on money, his exact due. He would have sworn before any court, earthly or celestial, that he had never crawled. The music ceased, and a flat, cultured voice began describing what had just been played. The woman cut the voice and returned the radio to her handbag. For a few seconds the café seemed to have gone dead; then he began to take in conversations, the clink of spoons, footsteps, cars going by: sounds so familiar that they amounted to silence. Of course he had begged. He had entreated for enough to eat, relief from pain, a passport, employment. Shreds of episodes shrugged off, left behind, strewed the roads. Only someone pledged to gray dawns would turn back to examine them. You might as well collect every letter you see lying stained in a gutter and call the assortment an autobiography.

There must have been some virtues, surely. For instance, he

had never tried to gain a benefit by fraud. Some people make a whole life out of trickery. They will even try to wrangle a box of the chocolates that the mayor of Paris distributes at Christmastime. These would-be swindlers may be in their fifties and sixties, too young to be put on the mayor's list. Or else they have a large income and really ought to pay for their own pleasures. Actually, it is the rich who put on shabby clothes and saunter into their local town hall, waving a gift voucher that wouldn't fool a child. And they could buy a ton of chocolates without feeling the squeeze!

The Wroblewskis, neither prosperous nor in want, get their annual gift in a correct and legal way. About four years ago, a notice arrived entitling Magda Zaleska, spouse Wroblewska, to the mayor's present. She was just beginning to show signs of alarm over quite simple matters, and so he went in her place, taking along her passport, a lease of which she was the co-signer, and a letter of explanation that he wrote and got her to endorse. (Nobody wanted to read it.) He remembers how he trudged upstairs and down before coming across a hand-lettered sign saying "Chocolates—Show Voucher and Identity."

The box turned out to be staggering in size, too large for a drawer or a kitchen shelf. It remained for weeks on top of the television set. (Neither of them cared for chocolate, except now and then a square of the bitter kind, taken with strong black coffee.) Finally, he transferred half the contents to a tin container that some Polish friends in England had used to send the Wroblewskis a gift of shortbread and digestive biscuits, and dispatched it to a distant cousin of Magda's. The cousin had replied that she could find chocolate in Warsaw but would welcome a package of detergent or some toilet soap that didn't take one's skin off.

He had used some of last year's chocolates as an offering for the concierge, packing them attractively in a wicker basket that had come with a purchase of dried apricots. She removed the ribbon and flowered paper, folded them, and exclaimed, "Ah!

The mayor's chocolates!" He still wonders how she knew: they are of excellent quality and look like any other chocolates you can see in a confectioner's window. Perhaps she is on the list, and sends hers off to relatives in Portugal. It hardly seems possible: they are intended for the elderly and deserving, and she is barely forty. Perhaps she is one of the schemers who has used deceit—a false birth certificate. What of it? She is a worthy woman, hardworking and kind. A man he knows of is said to have filed an affidavit that he was too badly off to be able to pay his yearly television tax and got away with it: here, in Paris, where every resident is supposed to be accounted for; where the entire life of every authorized immigrant is lodged inside a computer or crammed between the cardboard covers of a dossier held together with frayed cotton tape.

When he brings Magda her breakfast tray he looks as if he were on the way to an important meeting—with the bank manager, say, or the mayor himself. He holds to his side of the frontier between sleeping and waking, observes his own behavior for symptoms of contagion—haziness about time, forgetting names, straying from the point in conversation. He is fit, has good eyesight, can still hear the slide of letters when the concierge pushes them under the door. He was ten months in Dachau, the last winter and spring of the war, and lost a tooth for every month. They have been replaced, in an inexpensive, bric-a-brac way: better than nothing. The Germans give him a monthly pension, which covers his modest telephone bill, with a bit over. He is low on the scale of atonement. First of all, as the German lawyer who dealt with the claim pointed out, he was a grown man at the time. He had completed his education. He had a profession. One can teach a foreign language anywhere in the world. All he had to do when the war ended was carry on as before. He cannot plead that the ten months were an irreparable break, with a before and an after, or even a waste of life. When he explained about the German pension to a tax assessor, he was asked if he had served with the German Army. He feels dizzy if

138

he bends his head—for instance, over a newspaper spread flat—and he takes a green-and-white capsule every day, to steady his heart.

As soon as Marie-Louise rings the front doorbell, the dog drags the leash from its place in the vestibule and drops it at his feet. Hector is a young schnauzer with a wiry coat and a gamesome disposition, who was acquired on their doctor's advice as a focus of interest for Magda. He is bound to outlive his master. M. Wroblewski has made arrangements: the concierge will take him over. She can hardly wait. Sometimes she says to Hector, "Here we are, just the two of us," as if M. Wroblewski were already among the missing. Walking Hector seems to be more and more difficult. Parisians leave their cars along the curbs without an inch of space; beyond them traffic flies by like driven hail. When Magda, of all people, noticed that those few trees were missing, he felt unreasonable dismay, as if every last thing that mattered to him had been felled. Why don't they leave us alone? he thought. He had been holding silent conversations with no one in particular for some time. Then the letter came and he began addressing his friend. He avoids certain words, such as "problem," "difficulty," "catastrophe," and says instead, "A state of affairs."

The Nansen passports are being called in. Three people he knows, aged between eighty-one and eighty-eight, have had letters from the French Ministry for Foreign Affairs: the bureau that handles those rare and special passports is closing down. Polish political refugees do not exist any longer. They have been turned into Polish citizens (this is the first they've heard of it) and should apply to their own embassy for suitable documents. Two of the new citizens are an engraver, who still works in an unheatable studio on the far side of Montmartre, and another artist, a woman, who once modelled a strong, stunning likeness of Magda. She could not afford to have it cast, and the original got broken or was lost—he can't remember. It was through a work of art that he understood his wife's beauty. Until then he had been proud of her charm and distinction. He liked to watch her at the piano; he watched more than he listened, perhaps. The third is a former critic of Eastern European literature who at some point fell into a depression and gave up bothering with letters.

". . . and so, ipso facto, Polish citizens," the engraver told M. Wroblewski, over the telephone. "What are they going to do with us? Ship us back to Poland? Are we part of a quota now? At our age, we are better off stateless." Perhaps it is true. They never travel and do not need passports. Everyone has a place to live, an income of sorts. Two of the three still actually earn money. In a way, they look after one another.

No one has made a move. As the engraver says, when you are dealing with world-level bureaucracy, it is smarter to sit still. By the time you have decided how to react, all the rules may have been changed.

It is true and not true. One can quietly shift a pawn without causing a riot. M. Wroblewski's attitude runs to lines of defense. Probably, some clerk at the Ministry is striking off names in alphabetical order and is nowhere close to the "W"'s. After several false starts, he has written and mailed a letter to the Quai d'Orsay asking for French citizenship. He might have applied years ago, of course, but in the old days refusal was so consistent that one was discouraged at the outset. By the time he and Magda had their work, their apartment, their precious passports, the last thing they wanted was to fill in another form, stand in another line. He made no mention in the letter of refugees, status, or citizenship—other than French—but drew attention to the number of years he had lived in France, his fluent French, and his admiration for the culture. He spoke of the ancient historical links between Poland and France, touched briefly on the story of Napoleon and Mme. Waleska, and reminded the Ministry that he had never been behind with the rent or over-drawn at the bank.

(He sent the letter more than a month ago. So far, there has been no word from the Quai d'Orsay: an excellent sign. One can coast with perfect safety on official silence.)

In the meantime, something new has turned up. About three weeks ago he received a personal letter from the bank, written on a real typewriter, signed with real ink: no booklets, no leaflets, no pictures of a white-haired couple looking the Sphinx in the eye or enjoying Venice. There was just the personal message and one other thing, a certificate. "Certificate" was printed in thick black letters, along with his name, correctly spelled. A Mme. Carole Fournier, of Customers' Counselling Service, entreated him to sign the certificate, ask for an appointment, and bring it to her desk. (Her own signature seemed to him open and reliable, though still untried by life.) According to Mme. Fournier, and for reasons not made clear, he was among a handful of depositors—aristocrats, in their way—to whom the bank was proposing a cash credit of fifteen thousand francs. The credit was not a loan, not an overdraft, but a pool into which he could dip, without paying interest, any time he needed ready money but did not wish to touch his savings. The sums drawn from that fund would be replaced at the rate of two thousand francs a month, transferred from his current account. There was no interest or surcharge: he read that part twice.

For fifteen thousand francs he could fly to Australia, he supposed, or go on a cruise to the Caribbean. He could buy Magda a sumptuous fur coat. He would do none of those things, but the offer was generous and not to be rejected out of hand. He had opened an account with his first salary check in France: perhaps the bank wanted to show gratitude for years of loyalty. Besides his current account, he possessed two savings accounts. One of these is tax-free, limited by law to a deposit of fifteen thousand francs—by coincidence, the very amount he was being offered. Some people, he supposed, would grab the whole thing and dribble it away on nonsense, then feel downcast and remorseful as they watched their current account dwindle, month after month. The gift was a bright balloon with a long string attached.

141

The string could be passed from hand to hand—to the bank and back. He saw himself holding fast to the string.

Before he had a chance to do anything about it, he had a dizzy spell in the street and had to enter a private art gallery and ask to sit down. (They were not very nice about it. There was only one chair, occupied by a lady addressing envelopes.) His doctor ordered him to take a week's rest, preferably miles away from home. The preparation that was required—finding someone to sleep at the flat, two other people to come in during the afternoons and on the weekend—was more wearing than just keeping on; but he obeyed, left nothing undone, turned Hector over to the concierge, and caught the train for Saint-Malo. Years before, in an era of slow trains and chilly hotels, he had taken some of his students there. Uncomplaining, they ate dry sandwiches and apples and pitched the apple cores from the ramparts. This time he was alone in a wet season. Under a streaming umbrella he walked the ramparts again and when the sky cleared visited Chateaubriand's grave; and from the edge of the grave took the measure of the ocean. He had led his students here, too, and told them everything about Chateaubriand (everything they could take in) but did not say that Sartre had urinated on the grave. It might have made them laugh.

He left the grave and the sea and started back to the walled city. He thought of other violations and of the filth that can wash over quiet lives. In the dark afternoon the lighted windows seemed exclusive, like careless snubs. He would write to his friend, "I wondered what I was doing there, looking at other people's windows, when I have a home of my own." The next day he changed his train reservation and returned to Paris before the week was up.

Magda recognized him but did not know he had been away. She asked if he had been disturbed by the neighbor who played Schubert on the piano all night long. (Perhaps the musician existed, he sometimes thought, and only Magda could hear him.) "You must tell him to stop," she said. He promised he would.

# A State of Affairs

\*  \*  \*

Mme. Carole Fournier, Customers' Counselling Service, turned
out to be an attractive young woman, perhaps a bit thin in the
face. Her hollow cheeks gave her a birdlike appearance, but
when she turned to the computer screen beside her desk her
profile reminded him of an actress, Elzbieta Barszczewska.
When Barszczewska died, in her white wedding dress, at the end
of a film called *The Leper*, the whole of Warsaw went into
mourning. Compared with Barszczewska, Pola Negri was nothing.

The plastic rims of Mme. Fournier's glasses matched the two
red combs in her hair. Her office was a white cubicle with a large
window and no door. Her computer, like all those he had noticed in the bank, had a screen of azure. It suggested the infinite.
On its cerulean surface he could read, without straining, facts
about himself: his date of birth, for one. Between white lateral
blinds at the window he observed a bakery and the post office
where he bought stamps and sent letters. Hector, tied to a metal
bar among chained and padlocked bikes, was just out of sight.
Had the window been open, one might have heard his plaintive
barking. M. Wroblewski wanted to get up and make sure the
dog had not been kidnapped, but it would have meant interrupt-
ing the charming Mme. Fournier.

She glanced once more at the blue screen, then came back to
a four-page questionnaire on her desk. He had expected a welcome. So far, it had been an interrogation. "I am sorry," she
said. "It's my job. I have to ask you this. Are you sixty-six or
over?"

"I am flattered to think there could be any doubt in your
mind," he began. She seemed so young; his voice held a note of
teasing. She could have been a grandchild, if generations ran as
statistics want them to. He might have sent her picture to his
friend in Warsaw: red combs, small hands, zodiac (Gemini)
medallion on a chain. Across the street a boy came out of the

bakery carrying several long loaves, perhaps for a restaurant. She waited. How long had she been waiting? She held a pen poised over the questionnaire.

"I celebrated my sixty-sixth birthday on the day General de Gaulle died," he said. "I do not mean that I celebrated the death of that amazing man. It made me very sorry. I was at the theatre, with my wife. The play was *Ondine*, with Isabelle Adjani. It was her first important part. She must have been seventeen. She was the toast of Paris. Lovely. A nymph. After the curtain calls, the director of the theatre walked on, turned to the audience, and said the President was dead." She seemed still to be waiting. He continued, "The audience gasped. We filed out without speaking. My wife finally said, 'The poor man. And how sad, on your birthday.' I said, 'It is history.' We walked home in the rain. In those days one could walk in the street after midnight. There was no danger."

Her face had reflected understanding only at the mention of Isabelle Adjani. He felt bound to add, "I think I've made a mistake. It was not President de Gaulle after all. It was President Georges Pompidou whose death was announced in all the theatres of Paris. I am not sure about Adjani. My wife always kept theatre programs. I could look it up, if it interests you."

"It's about your being sixty-six or over," she said. "You'll have to take out a special insurance policy. It's to protect the bank, you see. It doesn't cost much."

"I am insured."

"I know. This is for the bank." She turned the questionnaire around so that he could read a boxed query: "Do you take medication on a daily basis?"

"Everyone my age takes something."

"Excuse me. I have to ask. Are you seriously ill?"

"A chronic complaint. Nothing dangerous." He put his hand over his heart.

She picked up the questionnaire, excused herself once more, and left him. On the screen he read the numbers of his three accounts, and the date when each had been opened. He remembered Hector, stood up, but before he could get to the window Mme. Fournier was back.

"I am sorry," she said. "I am sorry it is taking so long. Please sit down. I have to ask you another thing."

"I was trying to see my dog."

"About your chronic illness. Could you die suddenly?"

"I hope not."

"I've spoken to M. Giroud. You will need to have a medical examination. No, not by your own doctor," forestalling him. "A doctor from the insurance firm. It isn't for the bank. It is for them—the insurance." She was older than he had guessed. Embarrassment and its disguises tightened her face, put her at about thirty-five. The youthful signature was a decoy. "M. Wroblewski," she said, making a good stab at the consonants, "is it worth all this, for fifteen thousand francs? We would authorize an overdraft, if you needed one. But, of course, there would be interest to pay."

"I wanted the fund for the very reason you have just mentioned—in case I die suddenly. When I die, my accounts will be frozen, won't they? I'd like some cash for my wife. I thought I could make my doctor responsible. He could sign—anything. My wife is too ill to handle funeral arrangements, or to pay the people looking after her. It will take time before the will is settled."

"I'm sorry," she said. "I'm truly sorry. It is not an account. It is a cash reserve. If you die, it ceases to exist."

"A reserve of cash, in my name, held by a bank, is an account," he said. "I would never use or touch it in my lifetime."

"It isn't your money," she said. "Not in the way you think. I'm sorry. Excuse me. The letter should never have been sent to you."

"The bank knows my age. It is there, on the screen."

"I know. I'm sorry. I don't send these things out."

"But you sign them?"

"I don't send them out."

They shook hands. He adjusted his hat at a jaunty angle. Everything he had on that day looked new, even the silk ascot, gray with a small pattern of yellow, bought by Magda at Arnys, on the Rue de Sèvres—oh, fifteen years before. Nothing was frayed or faded. He never seemed to wear anything out. His nails were clipped, his hands unstained. He still smoked three Craven A a day, but had refrained in the presence of Mme. Fournier, having seen no ashtray on her desk. There had been nothing on it, actually, except the questionnaire. He ought to have brought her some chocolates; it troubled him to have overlooked a civility. He held nothing against her. She seemed competent, considerate in her conduct.

"Your accounts are in fine shape," she said. "That must be something off your mind. We could allow . . . At any rate, come back and see me if you have a problem."

"My problem is my own death," he said, smiling.

"You mustn't think such things." She touched her talisman, Gemini, as if it really could allow her a double life: one with vexations and one without. "Please excuse us. M. Giroud is sorry. So am I."


After the business about the letter and the Prussia question this morning, Magda was quiet. He let her finish her tea (she forgets she is holding a cup) and tried to draw her into conversation about the view from the window.

She said, "The neighbor is still playing Schubert all night. It keeps me awake. It is sad when he stops."

Their neighbors are a couple who go out to work. They turn off the television at ten and there is no further sound until half past six in the morning, when they listen to the news. At a quarter to eight they lock their front door and ring for the elevator, and the apartment is quiet again until suppertime. No one plays Schubert.

He picked up the tray. When he reached the doorway she said in a friendly, even voice, "The piano kept me awake."

"I know," he said. "The man playing Schubert."

"What man? Men can't play anything."

"A woman? Someone you know?"

He stood still, waiting. He said to his friend, If I get an answer, it means she is cured. But she will burrow under the blankets and pillows until Marie-Louise arrives. Once Marie-Louise is here, I will go out and meet you, or the thought of you, which never quits me now. I will read the news and you can tell me what it means. We will look at those mirrored walls across the boulevard and judge the day by colors: pale gold, gray, white-and-blue. A sheet of black glass means nothing: it is not a cloud or the sky. Let me explain. Give me time. From that distance, the dark has no power. It has no life of its own. It is a reflection.

Today I shall bring a pad of writing paper and a stamped, addressed envelope. You can think of me, at a table behind the window. (It is getting a bit cold for the street.) I have a young dog. As you can see, I am still boringly optimistic. Magda is well. This morning we talked about Schubert. I regret that your health is bad and you are unable to travel. Otherwise you could come here and we would rent a car and drive somewhere—you, Magda, the dog, and I. I am sorry about the radio talk and its effect on some low people. There are distorted minds here, too—you would not believe what goes on. Someone said, "Hitler lives!" at a meeting—so I am told. I suppose the police can't be everywhere. Please take good care of yourself. Your letters are precious to me. We have so many memories. Do you remember *The Leper*, and the scene where she dies at her own wedding? She was much more beautiful than Garbo or Dietrich—don't you think? I wish I had more to tell you, but my life is like the purring of a cat. If I were to describe it, it would put you to sleep. I may have more to tell you tomorrow. In the meantime, I send you God's favor.

# MLLE. DIAS DE CORTA

Y ou moved into my apart-
ment during the summer of
the year before abortion became legal in France; that should fix
it in past time for you, dear Mlle. Dias de Corta. You had just
arrived in Paris from your native city, which you kept insisting
was Marseilles, and were looking for work. You said you had
studied television-performance techniques at some provincial
school (we had never heard of the school, even though my son
had one or two actor friends) and received a diploma with "special mention" for vocal expression. The diploma was not among
the things we found in your suitcase, after you disappeared, but
my son recalled that you carried it in your handbag, in case you
had the good luck to sit next to a casting director on a bus.

   The next morning we had our first cordial conversation. I
described my husband's recent death and repeated his last
words, which had to do with my financial future and were not
overly optimistic. I felt his presence and still heard his voice in
my mind. He seemed to be in the kitchen, wondering what you

**149**

were doing there, summing you up: a thin, dark-eyed, noncommittal young woman, standing at the counter, bolting her breakfast. A bit sullen, perhaps; you refused the chair I had dragged in from the dining room. Careless, too. There were crumbs everywhere. You had spilled milk on the floor.

"Don't bother about the mess," I said. "I'm used to cleaning up after young people. I wait on my son, Robert, hand and foot." Actually, you had not made a move. I fetched the sponge mop from the broom closet, but when I asked you to step aside you started to choke on a crust. I waited quietly, then said, "My husband's illness was the result of eating too fast and never chewing his food." His silent voice told me I was wasting my time. True, but if I hadn't warned you I would have been guilty of withholding assistance from someone in danger. In our country, a refusal to help can be punished by law.

The only remark my son, Robert, made about you at the beginning was "She's too short for an actress." He was on the first step of his career climb in the public institution known then as Post, Telegrams, Telephones. Now it has been broken up and renamed with short, modern terms I can never keep in mind. (Not long ago I had the pleasure of visiting Robert in his new quarters. There is a screen or a machine of some kind everywhere you look. He shares a spacious office with two women. One was born in Martinique and can't pronounce her "r"s. The other looks Corsican.) He left home early every day and liked to spend his evenings with a set of new friends, none of whom seemed to have a mother. The misteachings of the seventies, which encouraged criticism of earlier generations, had warped his natural feelings. Once, as he was going out the door, I asked if he loved me. He said the answer was self-evident: we were closely related. His behavior changed entirely after his engagement and marriage to Anny Clarens, a young lady of mixed descent. (Two of her grandparents are Swiss.) She is employed in the accounting department of a large hospital and enjoys her work. She and Robert have three children: Bruno, Elodie, and Félicie.

# Mlle. Dias de Corta

It was for companionship rather than income that I had decided to open my home to a stranger. My notice in *Le Figaro* mentioned "young woman only," even though those concerned for my welfare, from coiffeur to concierge, had strongly counseled "young man." "Young man" was said to be neater, cleaner, quieter, and (except under special circumstances I need not go into) would not interfere in my relationship with my son. In fact, my son was seldom available for conversation and had never shown interest in exchanging ideas with a woman, not even one who had known him from birth.

You called from a telephone on a busy street. I could hear the coins jangling and traffic going by. Your voice was low-pitched and agreeable and, except for one or two vowel sounds, would have passed for educated French. I suppose no amount of coaching at a school in or near Marseilles could get the better of the southern "o," long where it should be short and clipped when it ought to be broad. But, then, the language was already in decline, owing to lax teaching standards and uncontrolled immigration. I admire your achievement and respect your handicaps, and I know Robert would say the same if he knew you were in my thoughts.

Your suitcase weighed next to nothing. I wondered if you owned warm clothes and if you even knew there could be such a thing as a wet summer. You might have seemed more at home basking in a lush garden than tramping the chilly streets in search of employment. I showed you the room—mine—with its two corner windows and long view down Avenue de Choisy. (I was to take Robert's and he was to sleep in the living room, on a couch.) At the far end of the Avenue, Asian colonization had begun: a few restaurants and stores selling rice bowls and embroidered slippers from Taiwan. (Since those days the community has spread into all the neighboring streets. Police keep out of the area, preferring to let the immigrants settle disputes in their own way. Apparently, they punish wrongdoers by throwing them off the Tolbiac Bridge. Robert has been told of a secret report, compiled by experts, which the Mayor has had on his desk for eighteen months. According to this report, by the year 2025 Asians will have taken over a third of Paris, Arabs and Africans three-quarters, and unskilled European immigrants two-fifths. Thousands of foreign-sounding names are deliberately "lost" by the authorities and never show up in telephone books or computer directories, to prevent us from knowing the true extent of their progress.)

I gave you the inventory and asked you to read it. You said you did not care what was in the room. I had to explain that the inventory was for me. Your signature, "Alda Dias de Corta," with its long loops and closed "a"s showed pride and secrecy. You promised not to damage or remove without permission a double bed, two pillows, and a bolster, a pair of blankets, a beige satin spread with hand-knotted silk fringe, a chaise longue of the same color, a wardrobe and a dozen hangers, a marble fireplace (ornamental), two sets of lined curtains and two of écru voile, a walnut bureau with four drawers, two framed etchings of cathedrals (Reims and Chartres), a bedside table, a small lamp with parchment shade, a Louis XVI–style writing desk, a folding card table and four chairs, a gilt-framed mirror, two wrought-iron wall fixtures fitted with electric candles and light bulbs shaped like flames, two medium-sized "Persian" rugs, and an electric heater, which had given useful service for six years but which you aged before its time by leaving it turned on all night. Robert insisted I include breakfast. He did not want it told around the building that we were cheap. What a lot of coffee, milk, bread, apricot jam, butter, and sugar you managed to put away! Yet you remained as thin as a matchstick and that great thatch of curly hair made your face seem smaller than ever.

You agreed to pay a monthly rent of fifty thousand francs for the room, cleaning of same, use of bathroom, electricity, gas (for heating baths and morning coffee), fresh sheets and towels once a week, and free latchkey. You were to keep a list of your phone calls and to settle up once a week. I offered to take messages and say positive things about you to prospective employers. The figure on the agreement was not fifty thousand, of course, but five hundred. To this day, I count in old francs—the denominations we used before General de Gaulle decided to delete two zeros, creating confusion for generations to come. Robert has to make out my income tax; otherwise, I give myself earnings in millions. He says I've had more than thirty years now to learn how to move a decimal, but a figure like "ten thousand francs" sounds more solid to me than "one hundred." I remember when a hundred francs was just the price of a croissant.

You remarked that five hundred was a lot for only a room. You had heard of studios going for six. But you did not have six hundred francs or five or even three, and after a while I took back my room and put you in Robert's, while he continued to sleep on the couch. Then you had no francs at all, and you exchanged beds with Robert, and, as it turned out, occasionally shared one. The arrangement—having you in the living room— never worked: it was hard to get you up in the morning, and the room looked as though five people were using it, all the time. We borrowed a folding bed and set it up at the far end of the hall, behind a screen, but you found the area noisy. The neighbors who lived upstairs used to go away for the weekend, leaving their dog. The concierge took it out twice a day, but the rest of the time it whined and barked, and at night it would scratch the floor. Apparently, this went on right over your head. I loaned you the earplugs my husband had used when his nerves were so bad. You complained that with your ears stopped up you could hear your own pulse beating. Given a choice, you preferred the dog.

I remember saying, "I'm afraid you must think we French are cruel to animals, Mlle. Dias de Corta, but I assure you not everyone is the same." You protested that you were French, too. I asked if you had a French passport. You said you had never applied for one. "Not even to go and visit your family?" I asked. You replied that the whole family lived in Marseilles. "But where were they born?" I said. "Where did they come from?"

There wasn't so much talk about European citizenship then. One felt free to wonder.

The couple with the dog moved away sometime in the eighties. Now the apartment is occupied by a woman with long, streaky, brass-colored hair. She wears the same coat, made of fake ocelot, year after year. Some people think the man she lives with is her son. If so, she had him at the age of twelve.


What I want to tell you about has to do with the present and the great joy and astonishment we felt when we saw you in the oven-cleanser commercial last night. It came on just at the end of the eight-o'clock news and before the debate on hepatitis. Robert and Anny were having dinner with me, without the children: Anny's mother had taken them to visit Euro Disney and was keeping them overnight. We had just started dessert— crème brûlée—when I recognized your voice. Robert stopped eating and said to Anny, "It's Alda. I'm sure it's Alda." Your face has changed in some indefinable manner that has nothing to do with time. Your smile seems whiter and wider; your hair is short and has a deep-mahogany tint that mature actresses often favor. Mine is still ash-blond, swept back, medium-long. Alain—the stylist I sent you to, all those years ago—gave it shape and color, once and for all, and I have never tampered with his creation.

Alain often asked for news of you after you vanished, mentioning you affectionately as "the little Carmencita," searching TV guides and magazines for a sign of your career. He thought you must have changed your name, perhaps to something short and easy to remember. I recall the way you wept and stormed after he cut your hair, saying he had charged two weeks' rent and cropped it so drastically that there wasn't a part you could audition for now except Hamlet. Alain retired after selling his salon to a competent and charming woman named Marie-Laure. She is thirty-seven and trying hard to have a baby. Apparently,

154

it is her fault, not the husband's. They have started her on hormones and I pray for her safety. It must seem strange to you to think of a woman bent on motherhood, but she has financial security with the salon (although she is still paying the bank). The husband is a car-insurance assessor.

The shot of your face at the oven door, seen as though the viewer were actually in the oven, seemed to me original and clever. (Anny said she had seen the same device in a commercial about refrigerators.) I wondered if the oven was a convenient height or if you were crouched on the floor. All we could see of you was your face, and the hand wielding the spray can. Your nails were beautifully lacquered holly-red, not a crack or chip. You assured us that the product did not leave a bad smell or seep into food or damage the ozone layer. Just as we had finished taking this in, you were replaced by a picture of bacteria, dead or dying, and the next thing we knew some man was driving you away in a Jaguar, all your household tasks behind you. Every movement of your body seemed to express freedom from care. What I could make out of your forehead, partly obscured by the mahogany-tinted locks, seemed smooth and unlined. It is only justice, for I had a happy childhood and a wonderful husband and a fine son, and I recall some of the things you told Robert about your early years. He was just twenty-two and easily moved to pity.

Anny reminded us of the exact date when we last had seen you: April 24, 1983. It was in the television film about the two friends, "Virginie" and "Camilla," and how they meet two interesting but very different men and accompany them on a holiday in Cannes. One of the men is a celebrated singer whose wife (not shown) has left him for some egocentric reason (not explained). The other is an architect with political connections. The singer does not know the architect has been using bribery and blackmail to obtain government contracts. Right at the beginning you make a mistake and choose the architect, having rejected the singer because of his social manner, diffident and shy. "Virginie" settles for the singer. It turns out that she has never heard of him and does not know he has sold millions of records. She has been working among the deprived in a remote mountain region, where reception is poor.

Anny found that part of the story hard to believe. As she said, even the most forlorn Alpine villages are equipped for winter tourists, and skiers won't stay in places where they can't watch the programs. At any rate, the singer is captivated by "Virginie," and the two sit in the hotel bar, which is dimly lighted, comparing their views and principles. While this is taking place, you, "Camilla," are upstairs in a flower-filled suite, making mad love with the architect. Then you and he have a big quarrel, because of his basic indifference to the real world, and you take a bunch of red roses out of a vase and throw them in his face. (I recognized your quick temper.) He brushes a torn leaf from his bare chest and picks up the telephone and says, "Madame is leaving the hotel. Send someone up for her luggage." In the next scene you are on the edge of a highway trying to get a lift to the airport. The architect has given you your air ticket but nothing for taxis.

Anny and Robert had not been married long, but she knew about you and how much you figured in our memories. She sympathized with your plight and thought it was undeserved. You had shown yourself to be objective and caring and could have been won round (by the architect) with a kind word. She wondered if you were playing your own life and if the incident at Cannes was part of a pattern of behavior. We were unable to say, inasmuch as you had vanished from our lives in the seventies. To me, you seemed not quite right for the part. You looked too quick and intelligent to be standing around with no clothes on, throwing flowers at a naked man, when you could have been putting on a designer dress and going out for dinner. Robert, who had been perfectly silent, said, "Alda was always hard to cast." It was a remark that must have come out of old café conversations, when he was still seeing actors. I had warned Anny he would be hard to live with. She took him on trust.

# Mlle. Dias de Corta

My husband took some people on trust, too, and he died disappointed. I once showed you the place on Place d'Italie where our restaurant used to be. After we had to sell it, it became a pizza restaurant, then a health-food store. What it is now I don't know. When I go by it I look the other way. Like you, he picked the wrong person. She was a regular lunchtime customer, as quiet as Anny; her husband did the talking. He seemed to be involved with the construction taking place around the Porte de Choisy and at that end of the Avenue. The Chinese were moving into these places as fast as they were available; they kept their promises and paid their bills, and it seemed like a wise investment. Something went wrong. The woman disappeared, and the husband retired to that seaside town in Portugal where all the exiled kings and queens used to live. Portugal is a coincidence: I am not implying any connection with you or your relations or fellow-citizens. If we are to create the Europe of the twenty-first century, we must show belief in one another and take our frustrated expectations as they come.

What I particularly admired, last night, was your pronunciation of "ozone." Where would you be if I hadn't kept after you about your "o"s? "Say 'Rhône,' " I used to tell you. "Not 'run.' " Watching you drive off in the Jaguar, I wondered if you had a thought to spare for Robert's old Renault. The day you went away together, after the only quarrel I ever had with my son, he threw your suitcase in the back seat. The suitcase was still there the next morning, when he came back alone. Later, he said he hadn't noticed it. The two of you had spent the night in the car, for you had no money and nowhere to go. There was barely room to sit. He drives a Citroën BX now.

I had been the first to spot your condition. You had an interview for a six-day modelling job—Rue des Rosiers, wholesale—and nothing to wear. I gave you one of my own dresses, which, of course, had to be taken in. You were thinner than ever and had lost your appetite for breakfast. You said you thought the apricot jam was making you sick. (I bought you some honey from Provence, but you threw that up, too.) I had finished basting the dress seams and was down on my knees, pinning the hem, when I suddenly put my hand flat on the front of the skirt and said, "How far along are you?" You burst into tears and said something I won't repeat. I said, "You should have thought of all that sooner. I can't help you. I'm sorry. It's against the law and, besides, I wouldn't know where to send you."

After the night in the Renault you went to a café, so that Robert could shave in the washroom. He said, "Why don't you start a conversation with that woman at the next table? She looks as if she might know." Sure enough, when he came back a few minutes later, your attention was turned to the stranger. She wrote something on the back of an old Métro ticket (the solution, most probably) and you put it away in your purse, perhaps next to the diploma. You seemed to him eager and hopeful and excited, as if you could see a better prospect than the six-day modelling job or the solution to your immediate difficulty or even a new kind of life—better than any you could offer each other. He walked straight out to the street, without stopping to speak, and came home. He refused to say a word to me, changed his clothes, and left for the day. A day like any other, in a way.

When the commercial ended we sat in silence. Then Anny got up and began to clear away the dessert no one had finished. The debate on hepatitis was now deeply engaged. Six or seven men who seemed to be strangling in their collars and ties sat at a round table, all of them yelling. The program presenter had lost control of the proceedings. One man shouted above the others that there were people who sincerely wanted to be ill. No amount of money poured into the health services could cure their muddled impulses. Certain impulses were as bad as any disease. Anny, still standing, cut off the sound (her only impatient act), and we watched the debaters opening and shutting their mouths. Speaking quietly, she said that life was a long duty, not a gift. She often thought about her own and had come to the conclusion that only through reincarnation would she ever know what she might have been or what important projects she might have carried out. Her temperament is Swiss. When she speaks, her genes are speaking.

I always expected you to come back for the suitcase. It is still here, high up on a shelf in the hall closet. We looked inside—not to pry but in case you had packed something perishable, such as a sandwich. There was a jumble of cotton garments and a pair of worn sandals and some other dresses I had pinned and basted for you, which you never sewed. Or sewed with such big, loose stitches that the seams came apart. (I had also given you a warm jacket with an embroidered Tyrolian-style collar. I think you had it on when you left.) On that first day, when I made the remark that your suitcase weighed next to nothing, you took it for a slight and said, "I am small and I wear small sizes." You looked about fifteen and had poor teeth and terrible posture.

The money you owed came to a hundred and fifty thousand francs, counted the old way, or one thousand five hundred in new francs. If we include accumulated inflation, it should amount to a million five hundred thousand; or, as you would probably prefer to put it, fifteen thousand. Inflation ran for years at 12 percent, but I think that over decades it must even out to ten. I base this on the fact that in 1970 half a dozen eggs were worth one new franc, while today one has to pay nine or ten. As for interest, I'm afraid it would be impossible to work out after so much time. It would depend on the year and the whims of this or that bank. There have been more prime ministers and annual budgets and unpleasant announcements and changes in rates than I can count. Actually, I don't want interest. To tell the truth, I don't want anything but the pleasure of seeing you and hearing from your own lips what you are proud of and what you regret.

My only regret is that my husband never would let me help in the restaurant. He wanted me to stay home and create a pleasant refuge for him and look after Robert. His own parents had slaved in their bistro, trying to please greedy and difficult people who couldn't be satisfied. He did not wish to have his only child do his homework in some dim corner between the bar and the kitchen door. But I could have been behind the bar, with Robert doing homework where I could keep an eye on him (instead of in his room with the door locked). I might have learned to handle cash and checks and work out tips in new francs and I might have noticed trouble coming, and taken steps.

I sang a lot when I was alone. I wasn't able to read music, but I could imitate anything I heard on records that suited my voice, airs by Delibes or Massenet. My muses were Lily Pons and Ninon Vallin. Probably you have never heard of them. They were before your time and are traditionally French.

According to Anny and Marie-Laure, fashions of the seventies are on the way back. Anny never buys herself anything, but Marie-Laure has several new outfits with softly draped skirts and jackets with a peasant motif—not unlike the clothes I gave you. If you like, I could make over anything in the suitcase to meet your social and professional demands. We could take up life where it was broken off, when I was on my knees, pinning the hem. We could say simple things that take the sting out of life, the way Anny does. You can come and fetch the suitcase any day, at any time. I am up and dressed by half past seven, and by a quarter to nine my home is ready for unexpected guests. There is an elevator in the building now. You won't have the five flights to climb. At the entrance to the building you will find a digit-code lock. The number that lets you in is K630. Be careful not to admit anyone who looks suspicious or threatening. If some stranger tries to push past just as you open the door, ask him what he wants and the name of the tenant he wishes to see. Probably he won't even try to give you a credible answer and will be scared away.

The concierge you knew stayed on for another fifteen years, then retired to live with her married daughter in Normandy. We

160

voted not to have her replaced. A team of cleaners comes in twice a month. They are never the same, so one never gets to know them. It does away with the need for a Christmas tip and you don't have the smell of cooking permeating the whole ground floor, but one misses the sense of security. You may remember that Mme. Julie was alert night and day, keeping track of everyone who came in and went out. There is no one now to bring mail to the door, ring the doorbell, make sure we are still alive. You will notice the row of mailboxes in the vestibule. Some of the older tenants won't put their full name on the box, just their initials. In their view, the name is no one's business. The postman knows who they are, but in summer, when a substitute makes the rounds, he just throws their letters on the floor. There are continual complaints. Not long ago, an intruder tore two or three boxes off the wall.

You will find no changes in the apartment. The inventory you once signed could still apply, if one erased the words "electric heater." Do not send a check—or, indeed, any communication. You need not call to make an appointment. I prefer to live in the expectation of hearing the elevator stop at my floor and then your ring, and of having you tell me you have come home.

# THE FENTON CHILD

## 1

I n a long room filled with cots and undesired infants, Nora Abbott had her first sight of Neil, who belonged to Mr. and Mrs. Boyd Fenton. The child was three months old but weedy for his age, with the face of an old man who has lost touch with his surroundings. The coarse, worn, oversized gown and socks the nuns had got him up in looked none too fresh. Four large safety pins held in place a chafing and voluminous diaper. His bedding—the whole nursery, in fact—smelled of ammonia and carbolic soap and in some way of distress.

Nora was seventeen and still did not know whether she liked children or saw them as part of a Catholic woman's fate. If they had to come along, then let them be clear-eyed and talcum-scented, affectionate and quick to learn. The eyes of the Fenton baby were opaquely grey, so rigidly focused that she said to herself, He is blind. They never warned me. But as she bent close, wondering if his gaze might alter, the combs at her temples slipped loose and she saw him take notice of the waves of dark hair that fell and enclosed him. So, he perceived things. For the rest, he remained as before, as still as a doll, with both hands folded tight.

Like a doll, yes, but not an attractive one: no little girl would have been glad to find him under a Christmas tree. The thought of a rebuffed and neglected toy touched Nora deeply. She lifted him from his cot, expecting—though not precisely—the limpness of a plush or woolly animal: a lamb, say. But he was braced and resistant, a wooden soldier, every inch of him tense. She placed him against her shoulder, her cheek to his head, saying, "There you go. You're just grand. You're a grand little boy." Except for a fringe of down around his forehead, he was perfectly bald. He must have spent his entire life, all three months of it, flat on his back with his hair rubbing off on the pillow.

In a narrow aisle between rows of beds, Mr. Fenton and a French-Canadian doctor stood at ease. Actually, Dr. Alex Marchand was a pal from Mr. Fenton's Montreal regiment. What they had in common was the recent war and the Italian campaign. Mr. Fenton appeared satisfied with the state and condition of his son. (With her free hand Nora pulled back her hair so he could see the baby entirely.) The men seemed to take no notice of the rest of the room: the sixty-odd puny infants, the heavily pregnant girl of about fourteen, waxing the floor on her hands and knees, or the nun standing by, watching hard to be sure they did not make off with the wrong child. The pregnant girl's hair had been cropped to the skull. She was dressed in a dun-colored uniform with long sleeves and prickly-looking black stockings. She never once looked up.

Although this was a hot and humid morning in late summer, real Montreal weather, the air a heavy vapor, the men wore three-piece dark suits, vest and all, and looked thoroughly formal and buttoned up. The doctor carried a Panama hat. Mr. Fenton had stuck a carnation in his lapel, broken off from a bunch he had presented to the Mother Superior downstairs, a few minutes before. His slightly rash approach to new people seemed to appeal. Greeting him, the nuns had been all smiles, accepting without shadow his alien presence, his confident ignorance of French, his male sins lightly borne. The liquor on his breath was enough to knock the Mother Superior off her feet (he was steady on his) but she may have taken it to be part of the natural aura of men.

"Well, Nora!" said Mr. Fenton, a lot louder than he needed to be. "You've got your baby."

What did he mean? A trained nanny was supposed to be on her way over from England. Nora was filling in, as a favor; that was all. He behaved as if they had known each other for years, had even suggested she call him "Boyd." (She had pretended not to hear.) His buoyant nature seemed to require a sort of fake complicity or comradeship from women, on short notice. It was his need, not Nora's, and in her mind she became all-denying. She was helping out because her father, who knew Mr. Fenton, had asked if she would, but nothing more. Mr. Fenton was in his late twenties, a married man, a father, some sort of Protestant—another race.

Luckily, neither the girl in uniform nor the attendant nun seemed to know English. They might otherwise have supposed Nora to be Neil's mother. She could not have been the mother of anyone. She had never let a man anywhere near. If ever she did, if ever she felt ready, he would be nothing like Mr. Fenton—typical Anglo-Montreal gladhander, the kind who said, "Great to see you!" and a minute later forgot you were alive. She still had no image of an acceptable lover (which meant husband) but rather of the kind she meant to avoid. For the moment, it took in just about every type and class. What her mother called "having relations" was a source of dirty stories for men and disgrace for girls. It brought bad luck down even on married couples unless, like the Fentons, they happened to be well-off and knew how to avoid accidents and had no religious barrier that kept them from using their knowledge. When a mistake did occur—namely, Neil—they weren't strapped for cash or extra space. Yet they were helpless in some other way, could not tend to an infant without outside assistance, and for that reason had left Neil to founder among castaways for his first twelve weeks.

So Nora reasoned, gently stroking the baby's back. She wondered if he had managed to capture her thoughts. Apparently infants came into the world with a gift for mind reading, an instinct that faded once they began to grasp the meaning of words. She had been assured it was true by her late Aunt Rosalie, a mother of four. The time had come to take him out of this sour place, see him fed, washed, put into new clothes and a clean bed. But the two men seemed like guests at a disastrous party, unable to get away, rooted in place by a purely social wish to seem agreeable.

How sappy they both look, ran Nora's thoughts. As sappy as a couple of tenors. ("Sappy-looking as a tenor" was an expression of her father's.) I'll never get married. Who wants to look at some sappy face the whole day.

As though he had heard every silent word and wished to prove he could be lively and attentive, the doctor looked all around the room, for the first time, and remarked, "Some of these children, it would be better for everybody if they died at birth." His English was exact and almost without accent, but had the singsong cadence of French Montreal. It came out, "Most of these children, it would be better for everybody . . ." Nora held a low opinion of that particular lilt. She had been raised in two languages. To get Nora to answer in French, particularly after she had started attending an English high school, her mother would pretend not to understand English. I may not be one of your intellectuals, Nora decided (an assurance her father gave freely), but I sound English in English and French in French. She knew it was wrong of her to criticize an educated man such as Dr. Marchand, but he had said a terrible thing. It would have sounded bad spoken heedfully by the King himself. (The King, that August morning, was still George the Sixth.)

The stiff drinks Mr. Fenton had taken earlier in the day must have been wearing off. He seemed faraway in his mind and somewhat put-upon. The doctor's remark brought him to. He said something about shoving off, turned easily to the nun, gave her a great smile. In answer, she placed a folded document in his hands, said a cool "*Au revoir*" to the doctor and did not look at Nora at all. In the hall outside Mr. Fenton stopped dead. He appealed to the doctor and Nora: "Look at this thing."

Nora shifted the baby to her right arm but otherwise kept her distance. "It's a certificate," she said.

"Baptismal," said the doctor. "He's been baptized."

"I can see that. Only, it's made out for 'Armand Albert Antoine.' She gave me the wrong thing. You'd better tell them," for of course he could not have made the complaint in French.

"Those are just foundling names," said the doctor. "They give two or three Christian names when there's no known family. I've seen even *four*. 'Albert' or 'Antoine' could be used as a surname. You see?"

"There damn well is a known family," said Mr. Fenton. "Mine. The name is Neil Boyd Fenton. When I make up my mind, it's made up for good. I never look back." But instead of returning the certificate he stuffed it, crumpled, into a pocket. "Nobody asked to have him christened here. I call that overstepping."

"They have to do it," said the doctor. "It is a rule." In the tone of someone trying to mend a quarrel, he went on, "Neil's a fine name." Nora knew for a fact he had suggested it. Mr. Fenton had never got round to finding a name, though he'd had three months to think it over. "There's another name I like. 'Earl.' Remember Earl Laine?"

"Yeah, I remember Earl." They started down a broad staircase, three in a row. Mr. Fenton was red in the face, either from his outburst or just the heat and weight of his dark clothes. Nora might have sympathized, but she had already decided not to do that: what can't be helped must be borne. Her mother had got her to wear a long-sleeved cotton jacket, over her white piqué dress, and a girdle and stockings, because of the nuns. The dress was short and allowed her knees to be seen. Nora had refused to let the hem down for just that one visit. Her small gold watch was a graduation present from her uncle and cousins. The blue bangle bracelets on her other wrist had belonged to her elder sister.

The mention of Earl Laine had started the men on a last-war story. She had already noticed their war stories made them laugh. They were not stories, properly speaking, but incidents they remembered by heart and told back and forth. Apparently, this Earl person had entered an Italian farmhouse ("shack" was the word Mr. Fenton actually used) and dragged a mattress off a bed. He wanted it for his tank, to make the tank more comfortable. A woman all in black had followed him out the door, clawing at the mattress, screaming something. When she saw there was no help for it, that Earl was bigger and stronger and laughing the whole time, she lay down in the road and thumped the ground with her fists.

"That Earl!" said the doctor, as one might speak of a bad but charming boy. "He'd do anything. Anything he felt like doing. Another time . . ."

"He was killed in '44," Mr. Fenton said. "Right? So how old would that make him now?"

It sounded very silly to Nora, like a conundrum in arithmetic, but the doctor replied, "He'd be around twenty-three." Dr. Marchand was older than Mr. Fenton but much younger than her father. He walked in a stately, deliberate way, like a mourner at a funeral. There was a wife-and-children air to him. Unlike Mr. Fenton he wore a wedding ring. Nora wondered if Mrs. Fenton and Mme. Marchand had ever met.

"Earl's people lived up in Montreal North," said Mr. Fenton. "I went to see them after I got back. They were Italians. Did you know that? He never said."

"I knew it the first time he opened his mouth," said the doctor. "His English wasn't right. It turned out his first language was some Sicilian dialect from Montreal North. Nobody in Italy could make it out, so he stayed with English. But it sounded funny."

"Not to me," said Mr. Fenton. "It was straight, plain Canadian."

The doctor had just been revealed as a man of deep learning. He understood different languages and dialects and knew every inch of Montreal far better than Nora or Mr. Fenton. He could construe a man's background from the sound of his words. No, no, he was not to be dismissed, whatever he had said or might still come out with. So Nora decided.

Downstairs, they followed a dark, waxed corridor to the front door, passing on the way a chapel recently vacated. The double doors, flung wide, revealed a sunstruck altar. Mr. Fenton's anti-papal carnations (Nora gave them this attribute with no hard feelings) stood in a vase of cut glass, which shed rainbows. A strong scent of incense accompanied the visitors to the foyer, where it mingled with furniture polish.

"Is today something special?" said Mr. Fenton.

A blank occurred in the doctor's long list of reliable information. He stared at the wall, at a clock with Roman numerals. Only the hour mattered, he seemed to be telling himself. Nora happened to know that today, the twenty-third of August, was the feast of Saint Rosa de Lima, but she could not recall how Saint Rosa had lived or died. Nora's Aunt Rosalie, deceased, leaving behind three sons and a daughter and sad Uncle Victor, had in her lifetime taken over any saint on the calendar with a Rose to her name: not just Saint Rosalie, whose feast day on September fourth was hers by right, but Saint Rosaline (January) and Saint Rosine (March) and Rosa de Lima (today.) It did not explain the special mass this morning; in any case, Nora would have thought it wrong to supply an answer the doctor could not provide.

Although someone was on permanent duty at the door, making sure no stranger to the place wandered in, another and much older nun had been sent to see them off. She was standing directly under the clock, both hands resting on a cane, her back as straight as a yardstick. Her eyes retained some of the bluish-green light that often goes with red hair. The poor woman most likely had not much hair to speak of, and whatever strands remained were bound to be dull and grey. The hair of nuns died early, for want of light and air. Nora's sister, Geraldine, had the same blue-green eyes but not yet the white circle around the iris. She was in the process now of suppressing and concealing her hair, and there was no one to say it was a shame, that her hair was her most stunning feature. So it would continue, unless Gerry changed her mind and came home to stay and let Nora give her a shampoo with pure white almond-oil soap, followed by a vinegar rinse. She would need to sit at the kitchen window and let the morning sun brighten and strengthen her hair to the roots.

The old nun addressed Mr. Fenton: "Your beautiful flowers are gracing our little chapel." At least, that was how Dr. Marchand decided to translate her words. Nora would have made it, "Your flowers are in the chapel," but that might have sounded abrupt, and "gracing" was undoubtedly more pleasing to Mr. Fenton.

"That's good to hear," he said. A current of laughter set off by the story of Earl and the mattress still ran in his voice. Nora was afraid he might pat the nun on the cheek, or in some other way embarrass them horribly, but all he did was glance up at the clock, then at his watch, and make a stagy sort of bow—not mockingly, just trying to show he was not in his customary habitat and could get away with a gesture done for effect. The clock struck the half hour: twelve-thirty. They should have been sitting down to lunch at Mr. Fenton's house, along with his wife and Mrs. Clopstock, who was his wife's mother. Nora had never before been invited to a meal at a strange table. This overwhelming act of hospitality was her reason for wearing white earrings, white high-heeled shoes and her sister's relinquished bracelets.

The hard midday light of the street stunned them quiet at first, then the baby set up a thin wail—his first message to Nora. I know, she told him. You're hungry, you're too hot. You need a good wash. You don't like being moved around. (For a second, she saw the hairline divide between being rescued and taken captive. The idea was too complex, it had no end or beginning, and she let it go.) You've dirtied yourself, too. In fact, you reek to high heaven. Never mind. We're going to put everything right. Trying to quiet him, she gave him one of her fingers to suck. Better to let him swallow a few germs and microbes than cry himself sick. Mr. Fenton had parked in shade, around the corner. It wasn't much of a walk.

"Nora can't remember the war," he said to the doctor, but really to her, trying the buddy business again. "She must have been in her cradle."

"I know it's over," she said, thinking to close the subject.

"Oh, it's that, all right." He sounded sorry, about as sorry as he could feel about anything.

The doctor had replaced his Panama hat, after three tries at achieving the angle he wanted. He made a reassuring sort of presence in the front seat—solid, reliable. Nothing would knock him over. Nora's father was thin and light as a blown leaf. The doctor said, "There's another name I like. Desmond."

"Des?" said Mr. Fenton. He struggled out of his jacket and vest and threw them on the backseat, next to Nora. His white carnation fell on the floor. The doctor remained fully dressed, every button fastened. "Des Butler?"

"He married an English girl," said the doctor. "Remember?"

"*Remember?* I was best man. She cried the whole time. She was called Beryl—no, Brenda."

"Well, she was in the family way," said the doctor.

"She hightailed it right back to England," said Mr. Fenton. "The Canadian taxpayers had to pay to bring her over. Nobody ever figured out where she got the money to go back. Even Des didn't know."

"Des never knew anything. He never knew what he should have known. All he noticed was she had gotten fat since the last time he saw her."

"She arrived with a bun in the oven," said Mr. Fenton. "Four,

**171**

five months. Des had already been back in Canada for six. So . . ." He turned his attention to Nora. "Your dad get overseas, Nora?"

"He tried."

"And?"

"He was already thirty-nine and he had the two children. They told him he was more useful sticking to his job."

"We needed civilians, too," said Mr. Fenton, showing generosity. "Two, did you say? Ray's got two kids?"

"There's my sister, Gerry—Geraldine. She's a novice now, up in the Laurentians."

"Where?" He twisted the rearview mirror, so he could see her.

"Near St. Jerome. She's on the way to being a nun."

That shut him up, for the time being. The doctor reached up and turned the mirror the other way. While they were speaking, the baby had started to gush up some awful curdled stuff, which she had to wipe on the skirt of his gown. He had no luggage—not even a spare diaper. The men had rolled down the front windows, but the crossbreeze was sluggish and smelled of warm metal, and did nothing to lighten the presence of Neil.

"Want to open up back there?" said Mr. Fenton.

No, she did not. One of her boy cousins had come down with an infected ear, the result of building a model airplane while sitting in a draft.

"At that stage, they're only a digestive tube," said the doctor, fanning himself with his hat.

"How about the brain?" said Mr. Fenton. "When does the brain start to work?" He drove without haste, as he did everything else. His elbow rested easily in the window frame. Ashes from his cigarette drifted into Nora's domain.

"The brain is still primitive," the doctor said, sounding sure. "It is still in the darkness of early time." Nora wondered what "the darkness of time" was supposed to mean. Mr. Fenton must have been wondering too. He started to say something, but the doctor went on in his slow singsong way, "Only the soul is fully developed from birth. The brain . . ."

"Newborn, they've got these huge peckers," said Mr. Fenton. "I mean, really developed."

"The brain tries to catch up with the soul. For most people, it's a lifelong struggle."

"If you say so, Alex," Mr. Fenton said.

The baby wasn't primitive, surely. She examined his face. There wasn't a hair on him except the blond fluff around his forehead. Primitive man, shaggy all over, dragged his steps through the recollection of a movie she had seen. Speak for yourself, she wanted to tell the doctor. Neil is not *primitive*. He just wants to understand where he's going. Her duty was to hand over to its mother this bit of a child, an only son without a stitch to his name. Socks, gown, and diaper were fit to be burned, not worth a washtub of water. So her sister had gone through an open door and the door had swung to behind her. She had left to Nora everything she owned. So Marie Antoinette, younger than Nora, had been stripped to the skin when she reached the border of France, on the way to marry a future king. Total strangers had been granted the right to see her nude. The clothes she had been wearing were left on the ground and she was arrayed in garments so heavy with silver and embroidery she could hardly walk. Her own ladies-in-waiting, who spoke her native language, were turned back. (Nora could not remember where Marie Antoinette had started out.) "For we brought nothing. . . ." Nora's Methodist Abbott grandmother liked to point out, convinced that Catholics never cracked a Bible and had to be kept informed. "Naked we came . . ." was along the same line. Nora knew how to dress and undress under a bathrobe, quick as a mouse. No earthquake, no burglar, no stranger suddenly pushing a door open would find Nora without at least one thing on, even if it was only a bra.

". . . from Mac McIvor," the doctor was telling Dr. Fenton. "He's out in Vancouver now. It's a big change from Montreal."

"He'll crawl back here one day, probably sooner than he thinks," said Mr. Fenton. Something had made him cranky, perhaps the talk about souls. "I consider it a privilege to live in Montreal. I was born on Crescent and that's where I intend to die. Unless there's another war. Then it's a toss-up."

"Crescent's a fine street," said the doctor. "Nice houses, nice stores." He paused and let the compliment sink in, a way of making peace. "He's buying a place. Property's cheap out there."

"It's a long way off," said Mr. Fenton. "They can't get people to go and live there. That's why everything's so cheap."

"Not being married, he doesn't need a lot of room," the doctor said. "It's just a bungalow, two rooms and a kitchen. He can eat in the kitchen. It's a nice area. A lot of gardens."

"Sure, there are stores on Crescent now, but they're high quality," said Mr. Fenton. "I could sell the house for a hell of a lot more than my father ever paid. Louise wants me to. She can't get used to having a dress shop next door. She wants a lawn and a yard and a lot of space between the houses."

"Mac's got a fair-size garden. That won't break his neck. Out there, there's no winter. You stick something in the ground, it grows."

"My father hung on to the house all through the Depression," said Mr. Fenton. "It'll take a lot more than a couple of store windows to chase me away." So saying, he made a sudden rough swerve into his street, having almost missed the corner.

It jolted the baby, who had just fallen asleep. Before he could start to cry or do anything else that could make him unpopular, she lifted him to the window. "See the houses?" she said. "One of them's yours." A few had fancy dress shops on the first floor. Others were turned into offices, with uncurtained front windows and neon lights, blazing away in broad daylight. The double row of houses ran straight down to St. Catherine Street without a break, except for some ashy lanes. Short of one of these, Mr. Fenton pulled up. He retrieved his vest and jacket, got out and slammed the door. It was the doctor who turned back to help Nora struggle out of the car, held her arm firmly, even adjusted the strap of her white shoulder bag. He wasn't trying anything, so she let him. Anyone could tell he was a family man.

Neil seemed more awkward to hold than before, perhaps because she was tired. Shielding his eyes from sunlight, she turned his face to a narrow house of pale grey stone. On her street, it would indicate three two-bedroom flats, not counting the area. She was about to ask, "Is the whole thing yours?" but it might make her sound as if she had never been anywhere, and the last thing she wanted was Mr. Fenton's entire attention. In the shadow of steps leading up to the front door, at a window in the area, a hand lifted a net curtain and let it fall. So, someone knew that Neil was here. For his sake, she took precedence and climbed straight to the door. The men barely noticed. Mr. Fenton, in shirt sleeves, vest and jacket slung over a shoulder, spoke of heat and thirst. Halfway up, the doctor paused and said, "Boyd, isn't that the alley where the girl was supposed to have been raped?"

"They never caught him," said Mr. Fenton at once. "It was dark. She didn't see his face. Some kids had shot out the alley light with an airgun. Her father tried to sue the city, because of the light. It didn't get him anywhere. Ray Abbott knows the story. Light or no light, it wasn't a city case."

"What was she doing by herself in a dark lane?" said the doctor. "Did she work around here?"

"She lived over on Bishop," said Mr. Fenton. "She was visiting some friend and took a shortcut home. Her father was a principal." He named the school. Nora had never heard of it.

"English," said Dr. Marchand, placing the story in context.

"They moved away. Some crazy stories went around, that she knew the guy, they had a date."

"I knew a case," said the doctor. "An old maid. She set the police on a married man. He never did anything worse than say hello."

"It was hard on Louise, something like that going on just outside. Nobody heard a thing until she ran down to the area and started banging on the door and screaming."

"Louise did that?"

"This girl. Missy let her in and gave her a big shot of brandy. Missy's a good head. She said, 'If you don't quit yelling I'll call the police.' "

"Her English must be pretty good now," said the doctor.

"Missy's smart. When my mother-in-law hired her, all she could say was, 'I cook, I clean.' Now she could argue a case in court. She told Louise, "Some guy grabs *me* in a lane, I twist him like a wet mop.' Louise couldn't get over it." He became light-hearted suddenly, which suited him better. "We shouldn't be scaring Nora with all this." Nora found that rich, considering the things that had been said in the car. She was at the door, waiting. He had to look up.

He took the last steps slowly. Of course, he was closer to thirty than twenty and not in great shape. All that booze and his lazy way of moving were bound to tell. On the landing he had to catch his breath. He said, "Don't worry, Nora. This end of Crescent is still good. It isn't as residential as when I was a kid but it's safe. Anyway, it's safe for girls who don't do dumb things."

"I'm not one for worrying," she said. "I don't wander around on my own after dark and I don't answer strangers. Anyways, I won't ever be spending the night here. My father doesn't like me to sleep away."

A word she knew but had never thought of using—"morose" —came to mind at the slow change in his face. Sulky or deeply pensive (it was hard to tell) he began searching the pockets of his vest and jacket, probably looking for his latchkey. The doctor reached across and pressed the doorbell. They heard it jangle inside the house. Without Dr. Marchand they might have remained stranded, waiting for the earth to turn and the slant of the sun to alter and allow them shade. Just as she was thinking this, wondering how Mr. Fenton managed to get through his day-by-day life without having the doctor there every minute, Dr. Marchand addressed her directly: *"On ne dit pas 'anyways.' C'est commun. Il faut toujours dire 'anyway.'"*

The heat of the day and the strain of events had pushed him off his rocker. There was no other explanation. Or maybe he believed he was some kind of bilingual marvel, a real work of art, standing there in his undertaker suit, wearing that dopey hat. Nora's father knew more about anything than he did, any day. He had information about local politics and the private dealings of men who were honored and admired, had their pictures in the *Gazette* and the *Star*. He could shake hands with anybody you cared to mention; could tell, just by looking at another man, what that man was worth. When he went to Blue Bonnets, the racetrack, a fantastic private intuition told him where to put his money. He often came home singing, his hat on the back of his head. He had an office to himself at City Hall, no duties anybody could figure, but unlimited use of a phone. He never picked a quarrel and never took offence. "Never let anyone get under your skin," he had told Gerry and Nora. "Consider the source."

She considered the source: Dr. Marchand had spent a horrible morning, probably, trying to sidestep Mr. Fenton's temporary moods and opinions. Still, the two of them were friends, like pals in a movie about the Great War, where actors pledged true loyalty in a trench before going over the top. Wars ran together, like the history of English kings, kept alive in tedious stories repeated by men. As a boring person he was easy to forgive. As a man he had a cold streak. His reproof stung. He had made her seem ignorant. Mr. Fenton didn't know a word of French, but he must have caught the drift.

Just as Nora's mother could predict a change in the weather from certain pains in her wrists, so the baby sensed a change in Nora. His face puckered. He let out some more of that clotted slobber, followed by a weak cough and a piercing, choking complaint. "Oh, stop," she said, hearing a rush of footsteps. She gave him a gentle shake. "Where's my little man? Where's my soldier?" Her piqué dress, which had been fresh as an ironed handkerchief just a few hours before, was stained, soiled, crumpled, wetted, damaged by Neil. She kissed his head. All she could find to say, in a hurry, was "Be good." The door swung open. Without being bidden Nora entered the house. The doctor removed his hat, this time with a bit of a flourish. Mr. Fenton, she noticed, was still looking for a key.

In rooms glimpsed from the entrance hall the shades were drawn against the burning street. A darker and clammier heat, like the air of an August night, condensed on her cheeks and forehead. She smiled at two women, dimly perceived. The younger had the figure of a stout child, wore her hair cut straight across her eyebrows and had on what Nora took to be a white skirt. In the seconds it took for her pupils to widen, her eyes to focus anew, she saw the white skirt was a white apron. In the meantime, she had approached the young woman, said, "Here's your sweet baby, Mrs. Fenton," and given him up.

"Well, Missy, you heard what Nora said," said Mr. Fenton. He could enjoy that kind of joke, laugh noisily at a mistake, but Missy looked as if a tide had receded, leaving her stranded and unable to recognize anything along the shore. All she could say was "There's a bottle ready," in a heavy accent.

"Give it to him right away," said the older woman, who could not be anyone but Mrs. Clopstock, the mother-in-law from Toronto. "That sounds to me like a hunger cry." Having made the observation, she took no further notice of Neil, but spoke to the two men: "Louise is really knocked out by the heat. She doesn't want any lunch. She said to say hello to you, Alex."

The doctor said, "Once she sees him, she'll take an interest. I had another case, just like that. I can tell you all about it."

"Yes, tell us Alex," said Mrs. Clopstock. "Do tell us. You can tell us about it at lunch. We have to talk about something."

It pleased Nora that Dr. Marchand, for the first time, had made a "th" mistake in English, saying "dat" for "that." He wasn't so smart, after all. Just the same, she had spoiled Neil's entrance into his new life; as if she had crossed the wrong line.

The two errors could not be matched. The doctor could always start over and get it right. For Nora and Neil, it had been once and for all.

2

Nora's uncle, Victor Cochefert, was the only member of her family, on either side, with much of consequence to leave in a will. He had the place he lived in—four bedrooms and double garage and a weeping willow on the lawn—and some flats he rented to the poor and improvident, in the east end of the city. He was forever having tenants evicted, and had had beer bottles thrown at his car. The flats had come to him through his marriage to Rosalie, daughter of a notary. Her father had drawn up a tight, grim marriage contract, putting Rosalie in charge of her assets, but she had suffered an early stroke, dragged one foot, and left everything up to Victor. The other relatives were lifelong renters, like most of Montreal. None were in want but only Victor and Rosalie had been to Florida.

Her own father's financial arrangements were seen by the Cocheferts as eccentric and somewhat obscure. He never opened his mouth about money but was suspected of being better off than he cared to let on; yet the Abbotts continued to live in a third-floor walkup flat, with an outside staircase and linoleum-covered floors on which scatter rugs slipped and slid underfoot. His wife's relations admired him for qualities they knew to exist behind his great wall of good humor; they had watched him saunter from the dark bureau where he had stood on the far side of a counter, wearing an eyeshade (against what light?), registering births and delivering certificates, to a private office in City Hall. He had moved along nonchalantly, whistling, hands in his pockets—sometimes in other people's, Victor had hinted. At the same time, he held Ray in high regard, knowing that if you

179

showed confidence, made him an accomplice, he could be trusted. He had even confided to Ray a copy of his will.

Victor's will was locked up in a safe in Ray's small office, where nothing was written on the door. "Nothing in the safe except my lunch," Ray often remarked, but Nora once had seen it wide open and had been impressed by the great number of files and dossiers inside. When she asked what these were, her father had laughed and said, "Multiple-risk insurance policies," and called her pie-face and sniffy-nose. She thought he must be proud to act as custodian to any part of Victor's private affairs. Victor was associate in a firm of engineers, established since 1900 on St. James Street West. The name of the company was Macfarlane, Macfarlane & Macklehurst. It was understood that when Macfarlane Senior died or retired, "Cochefert" would figure on the letterhead—a bit lower and to the right, in smaller print. Three other people with French surnames were on staff: a switchboard operator, a file clerk, and a bilingual typist. During working hours they were expected to speak English, even to one another. The elder Macfarlane harbored the fear that anything said in an unknown language could be about him.

Nora's father knew the exact reason why Uncle Victor had been hired: it had to do with Quebec provincial government contracts. Politicians liked to deal in French and in a manner they found pertinent and to the point. Victor used English when he had to, no more and no less, as he waited. He was waiting to see his name figure on the firm's stationery, and he pondered the retreat and obscuration of the English. "The English" had names such as O'Keefe, Murphy, Llewellyn, Morgan-Jones, Ferguson, MacNab, Hoefer, Oberkirch, Aarmgaard, Van Roos or Stavinsky. Language was the clue to native origin. He placed the Oberkirches and MacNabs by speech and according to the street where they chose to live. Nora's father had escaped his close judgment, was the English exception, even though no one knew what Ray thought or felt about anything. The well-known Anglo reluctance to show deep emotion might be a shield for something or for nothing. Victor had told his wife this, and she had repeated it to Nora's mother.

He had taken the last war to be an English contrivance and had said he would shoot his three sons rather than see them in uniform. The threat had caused Aunt Rosalie to burst into sobs, followed by the three sons, in turn, as though they were performing a round of weeping. The incident took place at a dinner given to celebrate the Cochefert grandparents' golden wedding anniversary—close relatives only, twenty-six place settings, small children perched on cushions or volumes of the Littré dictionary. The time was six days after the German invasion of Poland and three after Ray had tried to enlist. Victor was in such a state of pacifist conviction that he trembled all over. His horn-rimmed glasses fell in his plate. He said to Nora's father, "I don't mean this for you."

Ray said, "Well, in my family, if Canada goes to war, we go too," and left it at that. He spoke a sort of French he had picked up casually, which not everyone understood. Across the table he winked at Nora and Geraldine, as if to say, It's all a lot of hot air. His favorite tune was "Don't Let It Bother You." He could whistle it even if he lost money at Blue Bonnets.

Just before Victor's terrible outburst, the whole table had applauded the arrival of the superb five-tier, pink-and-white anniversary cake, trimmed with little gold bells. Now, it sat at the centre of the table and no one had the heart to cut it. The chance that one's children could be shot seemed not contrary to reason but prophetic. It was an unlucky age. The only one of Victor's progeny old enough to get into uniform and be gunned down by her father was his daughter, Ninon—Aunt Rosalie's Ninette. For years Victor and Rosalie had been alone with Ninette; then they had started having the boys. She was eighteen that September, just out of her convent school, could read and speak English, understand every word of Latin in the Mass, play anything you felt like hearing on the piano; in short, was ready to become a superior kind of wife. Her historical essay, "Marie-Antoinette,

Christian Queen and Royal Martyr," had won a graduation medal. Aunt Rosalie had brought the medal to the dinner, where it was passed around and examined on both sides. As for "Marie-Antoinette," Victor had had it printed on cream-colored paper and bound in royal blue, with three white fleurs-de-lys embossed on the cover, and had presented a copy to every person he was related to or wished to honor.

Nora was nine and had no idea what or where Poland might be. The shooting of her cousins by Uncle Victor lingered as a possibility but the wailing children were starting to seem a bit of a nuisance. Ninette stood up—not really a commanding presence, for she was small and slight—and said something about joining the armed forces and tramping around in boots. Since none of them could imagine a woman in uniform, it made them all more worried than ever; then they saw she had meant them to smile. Having restored the party to good humor, more or less, she moved around the table and made her little brothers stop making that noise, and cleaned their weepy, snotty faces. The three-year-old had crawled under the table, but Ninette pulled him out and sat him hard on his chair and tied his napkin around his neck, good and tight. She liked the boys to eat like grownups and remember every instructive thing she said: the Reverend Mother had told Victor she was a born teacher. If he would not allow her to take further training (he would not) he ought to let Ninette give private lessons, in French or music. Nothing was more conducive to moral disaster than a good female mind left to fester and rot. Keeping busy with lessons would prevent Ninette from dwelling on imponderables, such as where one's duty to parents ends and what was liable to happen on her wedding night. The Reverend Mother did not care how she talked to men. She was more circumspect with women, having high regard for only a few. Uncle Victor thought that was the best stand for the director of an exceptional convent school.

Having thoroughly daunted her little brothers, Ninette gave each of her troubled parents a kiss. She picked up a big silver cake knife—an 1889 wedding present, like the dictionary—and sliced the whole five-tier edifice from top to bottom. She must have been taught how to do it as part of her studies, for the cake did not fall apart or collapse. "There!" she said, as if life held nothing more to be settled. Before she began to serve the guests, in order, by age, she undid the black velvet ribbon holding her hair at the nape of her neck, and gave it to Geraldine. Nora watched Ninette closely during the cake operation. Her face in profile was self-contained, like a cat's. Ray had remarked once that all the Cochefert women, his own wife the single exception, grew a mustache by the age of eighteen. Ninette showed no trace of any, but Nora did perceive she had on mascara. Uncle Victor seemed not to have noticed. He wiped his glasses on his napkin and looked around humbly, as though all these people were too good for him, the way he always emerged from tantrums and tempers. He said nothing else about the war or the English, but as soon as he started to feel more like himself, remarked that it was no use educating women: it confused their outlook. He hoped Ray had no foolish and extravant plans for Nora and Geraldine. Ray went on eating quietly and steadily, and was first to finish his cake.

Nora's father was a convert, but he fitted in. He had found the change no more difficult than digging up iris to put in tulips. If something annoying occurred—say, some new saint he thought shouldn't even have been in the running—he would say, "I didn't sign on for that." Nora's mother had had a hard time with him over Assumption. He came from Prince Edward Island. Nora and Geraldine had been taken down there, just once, so Ray's mother could see her grandchildren. All her friends and neighbors seemed to be called Peters or White. Nora was glad to be an Abbott, because there weren't so many. They travelled by train, sitting up all night in their clothes, and were down to their last hard-boiled egg at the end of the journey. Their Abbott

**183**

grandmother said, "Three days of sandwiches." Of course it had not been anything like three days, but Nora and Gerry were trained not to contradict. (Their mother had made up her mind not to understand a word of English.)

Grandmother Abbott had curly hair, a striking shade of white, and a pink face. She wore quite nice shoes but had been forced to cut slits in them to accommodate her sore toes. Her apron strings could barely be tied, her waist was that thick around. She said to Gerry, "You take after your grandpa's side," because of the red-gold hair. The girls did not yet read English, and so she deduced they could not read at all. She told them how John Wesley and his brothers and sisters had each learned the alphabet on the day they turned five. It was achieved by dint of being shut up in a room with Mrs. Wesley, and receiving nothing to eat or drink until the recitation ran smoothly from A to Z.

"That's a Methodist birthday for you," said Ray. It may have stirred up memories, for he became snappy and critical, as he never was at home. He stood up for Quebec, saying there was a lot of good in a place where a man could have a beer whenever he felt like it, and no questions asked. In Quebec, you could buy beer in grocery stores. The rest of Canada was pretty dry, yet in those parched cities, on a Saturday night, even the telephone poles were reeling-drunk. Nora was proud of him for having all that to say. On their last evening a few things went wrong, and Ray said, "Tough corn and sour apple pie. That's no meal for a man." He was right. Her mother would never have served it. No wonder he had stayed in Montreal.


On a warm spring afternoon the war came to an end. Nora was fifteen and going to an English high school. She knew who George Washington was and the names of the Stuart kings but not much about Canada. A bunch of fatheads—Ray's assessment—swarmed downtown and broke some store windows and overturned a streetcar, to show how glad they felt about peace.

184

No one knew what to expect or what was supposed to happen without a war. Even Ray wasn't sure if his place on the city payroll was safe, with all the younger men coming back and shoving for priority. Uncle Victor decided to evict all his tenants, give the flats a coat of paint and rent them to veterans at a higher price. Ninette and Aunt Rosalie went to Eaton's and stood in one of the first lines for nylon stockings. Nora's mother welcomed the end of rationing on principle, although no one had gone without. Geraldine had been moping for years: she had yearned to be the youngest novice in universal history and now it was too late. Ray had kept saying, "Nothing doing. There's a war on." He wanted the family to stick together in case Canada was invaded, forgetting how eager he had been to leave at the very beginning, though it was true that in 1939 the entire war was expected to last about six months.

Now Gerry sat around weeping because she could leave home. When Ray said she had to wait another year, she suddenly stopped crying and began to sort the clothes and possessions she was giving up. The first thing she turned over to Nora was the black velvet ribbon Ninette had unfastened all those years ago. It was as good as new; Gerry never wore anything out. To Nora it seemed the relic of a distant age. The fashion now was curved combs and barrettes and hair clips studded with colored stones. Gerry went on separating her clothes into piles until the last minute and went away dry-eyed, leaving an empty bed in the room she had shared with Nora all Nora's life.

The next person to leave was Ninette. She came down with tuberculosis and had to be sent to a place in the Laurentians—not far from Gerry's convent. She never wrote, for fear of passing germs along by mail. If Nora wanted to send a letter, she had to give it, unsealed, to Aunt Rosalie. The excuse was that Ninette had to be shielded from bad news. Nora had no idea what the bad news might be. Ninette had never married. Her education had gone to waste, Nora often heard. She had inherited her father's habit of waiting, and now life had played her a mean trick. She had slapped her little brothers around for their own good and given private French lessons. Her favorite book was still her own "Marie-Antoinette." Perhaps she secretly had hoped to be martyred and admired. Ray had thought so: "The trouble with Ninette was all that goddamn queen stuff."

"Was," he had said. She had fallen into their past. After a short time Nora began to forget about her cousin. It was impossible to go on writing to someone who never replied. The family seemed to see less of Aunt Rosalie and Uncle Victor. Tuberculosis was a disgraceful disease, a curse of the poor, said to run through generations. Some distant, driven ancestor, a victim of winter and long stretches of émigré hunger had bequeathed the germ, across three centuries, perhaps. The least rumor concerning Ninette could blight the life of brothers and cousins. The summer after she vanished, Aunt Rosalie had a second stroke and two weeks later died.

One person who came well out of the war was Ray. He was in the same office, an adornment to the same payroll, and still had friends all over. He had devised a means of easing the sorrow of childless couples by bringing them together with newborn babies no one wanted to bring up. He had the satisfaction of performing a kindness, a Christian act, and the pleasure of experiencing favors returned. "Ray doesn't quite stand there with his hand out," Uncle Victor had been heard to say. "But a lot of the time he finds something in it." Ray had his own letter paper now, with "Cadaster/*Cadastre*" printed across the top. "Cadaster" had no connection to his job, as far as anyone could tell. He had found sheaves of the paper in a cardboard box, about to be carted away. The paper was yellowed and brittle around the edges. He enjoyed typing letters and signing his name in a long scrawl. He had once said he wanted his children to have names he could pronounce, and to be able to speak English at his own table if he felt like it. Both wishes had been granted. He was more cheerful than any man Nora had ever heard of and much happier than poor Uncle Victor.

Nora had to herself the room she had shared with her sister.

186

She placed Gerry's framed high-school graduation portrait on the dresser and kissed the glass, and spread her belongings in all the dresser drawers. Before long, her mother moved in and took over the empty bed. She was having her change of life and had to get up in the night to put on a fresh nightgown and replace the pillowcases soaked with sweat. After about a week of it, Ray came to the door and turned on the overhead light. He said, "How long is it going on for?"

"I don't know. Go back to bed. You need your sleep."

He walked away, leaving the light on. Nora went barefoot to switch it off. She said, "What does it feel like, exactly?"

Her mother's voice in the dark sounded girlish, like Gerry's. "As if somebody dipped a towel in boiling-hot water and threw it over your head."

"I'm never getting married," Nora said.

"Being married has nothing to do with it."

"Will it happen to Gerry?"

"Nuns get all the women's things," said her mother.

The August heat wave and her mother's restlessness kept Nora awake. She thought about the secretarial school where she was to begin a new, great phase of her life on the Tuesday after Labour Day—twelve days from tomorrow. Her imagination travelled along unknown corridors and into classrooms where there were rows of typewriters, just delivered from the factory; the pencils, the erasers, the spiral notebooks had never been touched. All the girls were attractive-looking and serious-minded. At a front-row desk (should they be seated in alphabetical order) was Miss Nora Abbott, with her natural bilingual skills and extensive wardrobe—half of it Gerry's.

As children, she and Gerry had taken parental magic on trust, had believed their mother heard their unspoken thoughts and listened from a distance to their most secret conversations. Now her mother said, "Can't you get to sleep, Nora? You're all impressed about taking that course. Are you wanting to leave home with your first pay cheque? Papa wouldn't want that."

"Gerry was eighteen when she went away."

"We knew where she was going."

"I'll be over nineteen by the time I start to work."

"And starting off at fifteen dollars a week, if you're lucky."

Nora said, "I've been wondering how Dad's going to manage to pay for the course. It's two hundred dollars, not counting the shorthand book."

"It's not for you to worry about," said her mother. "He's paid the hundred deposit. The rest isn't due until December."

"Uncle Victor had to chip in."

"Uncle Victor didn't *have* to do anything. When he helps out, it's because he wants to. Your father doesn't beg."

"Why couldn't he pay the whole hundred dollars on his own? Did he lose some of it at Blue Bonnets?"

Her mother sat up all of a sudden and became a looming presence in the dark. "Did you ever have to go bed on an empty stomach?" she said. "You and Gerry always had a new coat every winter."

"Gerry did. I got the hand-me-down. Grandma Abbott sent Gerry presents because she had red hair."

"Gerry's old coats looked as if they came straight from the store. She never got a spot or a stain on any of her clothes. Grandmother Abbott sent her a chocolate Easter egg once. It broke up in the mail and your father told her not to bother with any more parcels."

"Why would Uncle Victor have to lend Dad fifty dollars? What does he do with his money?"

"Did you ever have to go without shoes?" said her mother. "Did you ever miss a hot meal? Who gave you the gold chain and the twenty-four-carat crucifix for your First Communion?"

"Uncle Victor."

"Well, and who was he trying to be nice to? Your father. He's been the best father in the world and the best husband. If I go before he does, I want you to look after him."

I'll be married by then, Nora thought. "It's girls that look after their old dads," Ray had said when Victor had once commiserated with him for not having a son. Ninette was now back from the place in the Laurentians—cured, it was said—and had taken Aunt Rosalie's place, seeing to it that the boys did their homework and Uncle Victor got his meals on time. She wore her hair short (apparently the long hair had been taking all the strength) and had put on weight. Her manner had changed more than her appearance. She was twenty-six, unlikely to find a husband. A nagging, joyless religiosity had come over her. Nora had seen her only once since her return: Ninette had instructed Nora to pray for her, as though she were gradually growing used to giving spiritual orders. Nora had said to herself, She's like a sergeant-major. The whole family had been praying for Ninette for well over a year, without being pushed. Perhaps she had chosen this new, bossy way of behaving over another possibility, which was to sit with her head in her hands, thinking, Unfair! Either way, she was not good company.

Nora said to her mother, "You mean you want me to look after Dad the way Ninette takes care of Uncle Victor?"

"Poor Ninette," her mother said at once. "What else can she do now." Who would marry Ninette, she was trying to say. Ninette kept herself to herself; it may have been that one kept away from her—not unkindly, not dismissing the devaluation of her life, but for fear of ill luck and its terrible way of spreading by contact.

In the next room, Ray thumped on the wall and said, "Either we all get up and waltz or we pipe down and get some sleep."

Her last waking thoughts were about Gerry. When the time came to take over Ray's old age—for she had assumed her mother's wild requirement to be a prophecy—Gerry might decide to leave her convent and keep house for him. She could easily by then have had enough: Ray believed her vocation to be seriously undermined by a craving for peanut clusters and homemade fudge. In a letter she had run on about her mother's celebrated Queen of Sheba chocolate cake, artfully hollowed and filled with chocolate mousse and whipped cream. Nora tried to see Gerry and Ray: old and middle-aged, with Gerry trying to get him to drink some hot soup; her imagination went slack. Old persons were said to be demanding and difficult, but Gerry would show endless patience. Would she? Was she, any more than most people, enduring and calm? Nora could not remember. Only a year or so had gone by, but the span of separation had turned out to be longer and more effacing than ordinary time.

The next morning, and in spite of the heat, Ray requested pancakes and sausages for breakfast. No two of the Abbotts ever ate the same thing; Nora's mother stood on her feet until the family was satisfied. Then she cleared away plates, bowls, and coffee cups and made herself a pot of strong tea. Ray picked his teeth, and suddenly asked Nora if she wanted to do a favor for a couple he knew: it involved fetching this couple's baby and keeping an eye on it just a few hours a day, until the end of the week. The infant's mother had suffered a nervous breakdown at his birth, and the child had been placed in a home and cared for by nuns.

"Why can't they hire a nurse?" Nora said.

"She's on her way over from England. They're just asking you to be around till she comes. It's more than just a good turn," her father said. "It's a Christian act."

"A Christian act is one where you don't get paid," Nora said.

"Well, you've got nothing better to do for the moment," he said. "You wouldn't want to take money for this. If you take the money, you're a nursemaid and have to eat in the kitchen."

"I eat in the kitchen at home." She could not shake off the picture of Ray as old and being waited on by Gerry. "Do you know them?" she said to her mother, who was still standing, eating toast.

"Your mother doesn't know them," said Ray.

"I just saw the husband once," said his wife. "It was around the time when Ninette had to stop giving lessons. Mrs. Fenton used to come once a week. She must have started being de-

190

pressed before the baby came along, because she couldn't concentrate or remember anything. Taking lessons was supposed to pull her mind together. He brought a book belonging to Ninette and I think he paid for some lessons his wife still owed. Ninette wasn't around. Aunt Rosalie introduced us. That was all."

"You never told me about that," said Ray.

"What was he like?" said Nora.

Her mother answered, in English, "Like an English."


Nora and her father took the streetcar down to the stone building where Ray had worked before moving into his office at City Hall. He put on his old green eyeshade and got behind an oak counter. He was having a good time, playing the role of a much younger Ray Abbott, knowing all the while he had the office and the safe and connections worth a gold mine. Mr. Fenton and his doctor friend were already waiting, smoking under a dilapidated NO SMOKING sign. Nora felt not so much shy as careful. She took in their light hot-weather clothes—the doctor's pale beige jacket, with wide lapels, and Mr. Fenton's American-looking seersucker. The huge room was dark and smelled of old books and papers. It was not the smell of dirt, though the place could have done with a good cleanout.

Nora and the men stood side by side, across from her father. Another person, whom she took to be a regular employee, was sitting at a desk, reading the *Gazette* and eating a Danish. Her father had in front of him a ledger of printed forms. He filled in the blank spaces by hand, using a pen, which he dipped with care in black ink. Mr. Fenton dictated the facts. Before giving the child's name or its date of birth, he identified his wife and, of course, himself: they were Louise Marjorie Clopstock and Boyd Markham Forrest Fenton. He was one of those Anglos with no Christian name, just a string of surnames. Ray lifted the pen over the most important entry. He peered up, merry-looking as a squirrel. It was clear that Mr. Fenton either could not remember or make up his mind. "Scott?" he said, as if Ray ought to know.

The doctor said, "Neil Boyd Fenton," pausing heavily between syllables.

"Not Neil Scott?"

"You said you wanted 'Neil Boyd.'"

Nora thought, You'd think Dr. Marchand was the mother.
Ray wrote the name carefully and slowly, and the date of birth.
Reading upside down, she saw that the Fenton child was three
months old, which surely was past the legal limit of registration.
Her father turned the ledger around so Mr. Fenton could sign,
and said, "Hey, Vince," to the man eating Danish. He came over
and signed too, and then it was the doctor's turn.

Mr. Fenton said, "Shouldn't Nora be a witness?" and her
father said, "I think we could use an endorsement from the little
lady," as if he had never seen her before. To the best of Nora's
knowledge, all the information recorded was true, and so she
signed her name to it, along with the rest.

Her father sat down where Vince had been, brushed away
some crumbs, and ran a cream-colored document into a big
clackety typewriter, older than Nora, most likely. When he had
finished repeating the names and dates in the ledger, he fastened
a red seal to the certificate and brought it back to the counter to
be signed. The same witnesses wrote their names, but only Nora,
it seemed, saw her father's mistakes: he had typed "Nell" for
"Neil" and "Frenton" for "Fenton" and had got the date of
birth wrong by a year, giving "Nell Frenton" the age of fifteen
months. The men signed the certificate without reading it. If she
and her father had been alone, she could have pointed out the
mistakes, but of course she could not show him up in front of
strangers.

The doctor put his fountain pen away and remarked, "I like
Neil for a name." He spoke to Mr. Fenton in English and to Ray
and Nora not at all. At the same time he and Nora's father
seemed to know each other. There was an easiness of acquaintance between them; a bit cagey perhaps. Mr. Fenton seemed
more like the sort of man her father might go with to the races.
She could imagine them easily going on about bets and horses.

Most of the babies Ray was kind enough to find for unhappy couples were made known by doctors. Perhaps he was one of them.

It was decided between Ray and Mr. Fenton that Nora would be called for, the next morning, by Mr. Fenton and the doctor. They would all three collect the child and take him home. Nora was invited to lunch. Saying goodbye, Mr. Fenton touched her bare arm, perhaps by accident, and asked her to call him "Boyd." Nothing in her manner or expression showed she had heard.

That evening, Ray and his wife played cards in the kitchen. Nora was ironing the starched piqué dress she would wear the next day. She said, "They gave up their own baby for adoption, or what?"

"Maybe they weren't expecting a child. It was too much for them," her mother said.

"Give us a break," said Ray. "Mrs. Fenton wasn't in any shape to look after him. She had *her* mother down from Toronto because she couldn't even run the house. They've got this D.P. maid always threatening to quit."

"Does he mind having his mother-in-law around the whole time?" said Nora.

"He sure doesn't." Nora thought he would add some utterly English thing, like "She's got the money," but Ray went on, "She's on his side. She wants them together. The baby's the best thing that could happen."

"Maybe there was a mistake at the hospital," said Nora's mother, trying again. "The Fentons got some orphan by mistake and their own baby went to the home."

"And then the truth came out," said Nora. It made sense.

"Now when you're over there, don't you hang out with that maid," Ray said. "She can't even speak English. If somebody says to you to eat in the kitchen, I want you to come straight home."

"I'm not leaving home," said Nora. "I'm not sure if I want to go back to their place after tomorrow."

"Come on," said Ray. "I promised."

"You promised. I didn't."

"Leave your dress on the ironing board," said her mother. "I'll do the pleats."

Nora switched off the iron and went to stand behind her father. She put her hands on his shoulders. "Don't worry," she said. "I'm not going to let you down. You might as well throw your hand in. I saw Maman's."

### 3

Obliged to take the baby from Nora, Missy now held him at arm's length, upright between her hands, so that no part of him could touch her white apron. Nora thought, He'll die from his own screaming. Missy's face said she was not enjoying the joke. Perhaps she thought Mr. Fenton had put Nora up to it. His laughter had said something different: whatever blunders he might have committed until now, choosing Missy to be the mother of a Fenton was not among them.

"You'd better clean him up right away," said Mrs. Clopstock.

Missy, whose silences were astonishingly powerful, managed to suggest that cleaning Neil up was not in her working agreement. She did repeat that a bottle was ready for some reason, staring hard at the doctor.

"The child is badly dehydrated," he said, as if replying to Missy. "He should be given liquid right away. He is undernourished and seriously below his normal weight. As you can tell, he has a bad case of diarrhea. I'll take his temperature after lunch."

"Is he really sick?" said Nora.

"He may have to be hospitalized for a few days." He was increasingly solemn and slower than ever.

"Hospitalized?" said Mr. Fenton. "We've only just got him here."

"The first thing is to get him washed and changed," said Mrs. Clopstock.

"I'll do it," said Nora. "He knows me."

"Missy won't mind."

Sensing a private exchange between Mrs. Clopstock and Missy, Nora held still. She felt a child's powerful desire to go home, away from these strangers. Mrs. Clopstock said, "Let us all please go and sit down. We're standing here as if we were in a hotel lobby."

"I can do it," Nora said. She said again, "He knows me."

"Missy knows where everything is," said Mrs. Clopstock. "Come along, Alex, Boyd. Nora, don't you want to wash your hands?"

"I'm feeling dehydrated too," said Mr. Fenton. "I hope Missy put something on ice."

Nora watched Missy turn and climb the stairs, and disappear around the bend in the staircase. There'll be a holy row about this, she thought. I'll be gone.

"It was very nice meeting you," she said. "I have to leave now."

"Come on, Nora," said Mr. Fenton. "Anybody could have made the same mistake. You came in out of bright sunlight. The hall was dark."

"Could we please, please go and sit down?" said his mother-in-law.

"All right," he said, still to Nora. "It's O.K. You've had enough. Let's have a bite to eat and I'll drive you home."

"You may have to take Neil to the hospital."

Mrs. Clopstock took the doctor's arm. She was a little woman in green linen, wearing pearls and pearl earrings. Aunt Rosalie would have seen right away if they were real. The two moved from the shaded hall to a shaded room.

Mr. Fenton watched them go. "Nora," he said, "just let me have a drink and I'll drive you home."

**195**

"I don't need to be driven home. I can take the Sherbrooke bus and walk the rest of the way."

"Can you tell me what's wrong? It can't be my mother-in-law. She's a nice woman. Missy's a little rough, but she's nice too."

"Where's Mrs. Fenton?" said Nora. "Why didn't she at least come to the door? It's her child."

"You're not dumb," he said. "You're not Ray's girl for nothing. It's hers and it isn't."

"We all signed," Nora said. "I didn't sign to cover up some story. I came here to do a Christian act. I wasn't paid anything."

"What do you mean by 'anything'? You mean not enough?"

"Who's Neil?" she said. "I mean, who *is* he?"

"He's a Fenton. You saw the register."

"I mean, *who* is he?"

"He's my son. You signed the register. You should know."

"I believe you," she said. "He has English eyes." Her voice dropped. He had to ask her to repeat something. "I said, was it Ninette?"

It took him a second or so to see what she was after. He gave the same kind of noisy laugh as when she had tried to place the child in Missy's arms. "Little Miss Cochefert? Until this minute I thought you were the only sane person in Montreal."

"It fits," said Nora. "I'm sorry."

"Well, I'll tell you," he said. "I don't know. There are two people that know. Your father, Ray Abbott and Alex Marchand."

"Did you pay my Dad?"

"*Pay* him? I paid him for *you*. We wouldn't have asked anyone to look after Neil for nothing."

"About Ninette," she said. "I just meant that it fits."

"A hundred women in Montreal would fit, when it comes to that. The truth is, we don't know, except that she was in good health."

"Who was the girl in the lane? The one you were talking about."

"Just a girl in the wrong place. Her father was a school principal."

"You said that. Did you know her?"

"I never saw her. Missy and Louise did. Louise is my wife."

"I know. How much did you give my dad? Not for Neil. For
me."

"Thirty bucks. Some men don't make that in a week. If you
have to ask, it means you never got it."

"I've never had thirty dollars in one piece in my life," she said.
"In my family we don't fight over money. What my dad says,
goes. I've never had to go without. Gerry and I had new coats
every winter."

"Is that the end of the interrogatory? You'd have made a great
cop. I agree, you can't stay. But would you just do one last
Christian act? Wash your hands and comb your hair and sit
down and have lunch. After that, I'll put you in a taxi and pay
the driver. If you don't want me to, my mother-in-law will."

"I could help you take him to the hospital."

"Forget the Fenton family," he said. "Lunch is the cutoff."


Late in the afternoon Ray came home and they had tea and
sandwiches at the kitchen table. Nora was wearing Gerry's old
white terrycloth robe. Her washed hair was in rollers.

"There was nothing to it, no problem," she said again. "He
needed a hospital checkup. He was run-down. I don't know
which hospital."

"I could find out," said Ray.

"I think they don't want anybody around."

"What did you eat for lunch?" said her mother.

"Some kind of cold soup. Some kind of cold meat. A fruit
salad. Iced tea. The men drank beer. There was no bread on the
table."

"Pass Nora the peanut butter," said Ray.

"Did you meet Mr. Fenton because of Ninette," said Nora,

"or did you know him first? Did you know Dr. Marchand first, or Mr. Fenton?"

"It's a small world," said her father. "Anyways, I've got some money for you."

"How much?" said Nora. "No, never mind. I'll ask if I ever need it."

"You'll never need anything," he said. "Not as long as your old dad's around."

"You know, that Mrs. Clopstock?" said Nora. "She's the first person I've ever met from Toronto. I didn't stare at her, but I took a good look. Maman, how can you tell real pearls?"

"They wouldn't be real," said Ray. "The real ones would be on deposit. Rosalie had a string of pearls."

"They had to sell them on account of Ninette," said her mother.

"Maybe you could find out the name of the hospital," Nora said. "He might like to see me. He knows me."

"He's already forgotten you," her mother said.

"I wouldn't swear to that," said Ray. "I can remember somebody bending over my baby buggy. I don't know who it was, though."

He will remember that I picked him up, Nora decided. He will remember the smell of the incense. He will remember the front door and moving into the dark hall. I'll try to remember him. It's the best I can do.

She said to Ray, "What's the exact truth? Just what's on paper?"

"Nora," said her mother. "Look at me. Look me right in the face. Forget that child. He isn't yours. If you want children, get married. All right?"

"All right," her father answered for her. "Why don't you put on some clothes and I'll take you both to a movie." He began to whistle, not "Don't Let It Bother You," but some other thing just as easy.

198